The Ripple Effect

Brenden Boyer

Contents

1.	Chapter 1	1
2.	Chapter 2	9
3.	Chapter 3	13
4.	Chapter 4	23
5.	Chapter 5	33
6.	Chapter 6	39
7.	Chapter 7	49
8.	Chapter 8	55
9.	Chapter 9	60
10.	Chapter 10	69
11.	Chapter 11	72
12.	Chapter 12	77
13.	Chapter 13	83
14.	Chapter 14	85
15.	Chapter 15	90
16.	Chapter 16	92
17.	Chapter 17	95

18. Chapter 18   98

19. Chapter 19   104

20. Chapter 20   108

21. Chapter 21   111

22. Chapter 22   114

23. Chapter 23   121

24. Chapter 24   124

25. Chapter 25   128

26. Chapter 26   133

27. Chapter 27   137

28. Chapter 28   141

29. Chapter 29   143

30. Epilogue   150

Chapter 1

T he day I first spoke to him began like any other day. I woke up late and was rushing to get ready for school, all while my dad yelled up the stairs at me that I was going to be late. I always rolled my eyes when he felt the need to say that. I already knew I was going to be late; that's why I was rushing. It never took long before I was ready and running down the stairs. I always yelled "Bye" at my parents as I ran out the door and to my car. That day was no different.

The drive to school was a short one, so it wasn't long before I was parked and made my way into the building. I still had a few minutes before class started. I had time to stop at my locker, loop arms with a friend who shared first period, and head to the classroom. We were seated with a minute to spare.

"Wow, Dee. You really like to cut it close."

I turned my head to look at my friend. I rolled my eyes and responded, "Violet, class hasn't started, and Ms. Mahoney is nowhere to be seen. It's fine."

Violet laughed and turned to face forward. "You really have no fear when it comes to school. Do you, Delta?"

I looked over her face before turning to face forward as well. "Why should I be afraid of anyone or any consequences here? The people and time here are a brief moment of my life. It's all irrelevant."

I glanced over at Violet, who was looking at me with a smirk. "So, after graduation, you're just going to go on with your life and forget all about me and the rest of our friends?"

The corners of my lips twitched upward in a smirk. "Well, if you're lucky, I'll keep in touch with you, Vi."

She laughed and shook her head. "Screw you, Novak."

"You know you love me," I mumbled back and looked down at my desk.

Classes went by quickly, and before I knew it, it was time for lunch. Lunch was the best time of day. It was the only time during school hours that I was together with all my friends. I rushed up to the table that seated my group and slid in next to Violet, bumping roughly into her. She shoved me over and loudly stated, "Guys, guess what. After graduation, Dee is going to move on from this little town and leave all of us behind, without a second thought about it."

Scarlet rolled her eyes and, with one hand, flipped her hair behind her shoulder. "So what? Dee is just as insignificant as the rest of us."

Scarlet was what some might call the leader of our small group of friends. She was a bold girl, who never felt the need to spare anyone's feelings. She was icy and blunt, and the word "sorry" was not in her vocabulary. She was known most throughout the school as being a bitch. More specifically, people often said, in reference to Scarlet, "She's a self-centered ice queen who will die alone for being such an intolerable bitch." Scarlet had plenty of negative qualities that should have made her unlikable, but for whatever reason, everyone in our group liked her despite those flaws.

"Ooo harsh!" Marco exclaimed.

I smirked and held up my middle finger to Scarlet before saying, "Everyone on this earth is insignificant after enough time passes."

Joshua raised an eyebrow at me, then nodded. "That was unexpectedly deep."

Joshua and Marco were twins. They lived a few houses down from me, and the three of us had been friends our whole lives. Marco was commonly referred to as a clown or a goofball. He rarely took anything seriously, and he always viewed the world with a positive lens. Joshua was far more serious when compared with his brother. Joshua had more of a dark side, and throughout the years, he had been bullied for being "emo." Coming into high school, Joshua stopped dressing in all black and started taking medication for his insomnia. Now he's seen as one of the hottest guys in our high school, and he's become fairly popular.

I rolled my eyes and casually said, "I'm very deep, Joshy. I have layers upon layers."

Marco looked at me with furrowed eyebrows. "Are you saying you're an onion?"

I looked at Marco in a way that suggested I was questioning whether he had any brain cells. "Why the hell would that mean I'm an onion?"

Marco looked around the table to be met with looks similar to the one I was giving him. He hesitantly said, "Well, when Shrek said it, he said that he was like an onion."

Violet started laughing at an obnoxious volume. "Dude, he just called you Shrek."

"No, Marco. I'm not a damn onion."

Before the onion conversation could continue, the bell rang, announcing the end of the lunch period. We all began gathering our trash, and I threw an annoyed look at Marco. We headed to the exit of the cafeteria as a group, and we each threw away our trash as we exited through the large double doors.

"What classes does everyone have?" Violet shouted out to all of us.

Everyone began speaking over each other. I couldn't make out what anyone said except for Joshua, who was walking next to me. He mumbled out that he had English next. I bumped his should with mine and said, "I have English too. Sit together?"

He smirked at me and said, "I'd never miss out on an opportunity to sit next to you."

I smiled back at him. "I am pretty great, aren't I?"

"You're something, but I don't know if I'd call it great."

I rolled my eyes and shoved him with a smile. "Shut it."

He laughed, and we continued to English together.

Though neither of us were open about it, Joshua and I had shared a favorite subject in English. We both loved literature—more specifically, poetry. Joshua started writing poetry to cope with the bullying when we were growing up. It was something that he had always kept secret. I had stumbled upon it when he lent me the wrong notebook in our freshman year. He was nervous about how I would react, but he was relieved when I supported his hobby. After that, he began asking me to help him edit anything he wrote.

The class period was spent reviewing the course syllabus and discussing the upcoming assignments. After the introduction to the course work, we were left to talk amongst ourselves or begin working ahead. Joshua and I sat in the back corner of the class, and we quietly discussed the upcoming assignments. We enjoyed brainstorming ideas for writing assignments, but we did our best to hide our enthusiasm.

As we made plans for Joshua to come over after school to discuss everything more in depth, a wadded up piece of paper hit Joshua in the face and fell onto his desk. I frowned at him and turned in the direction the paper ball had come from. There were two boys laughing while a third watched them with a bored expression.

I looked back at Joshua, who had flattened out the piece of paper. "What does it say?"

A dark chuckle escaped his lips as he shook his head. "Nothing."

I reached out and snatched the piece of paper from him just as the bell rang. I clenched my jaw as I read the paper.

"Kill yourself Jock"

I quickly stood up and scanned through the people left in the classroom. The three boys from earlier were already gone. I quickly made my way out of the classroom with Joshua chasing after me, calling out my name. I found the three boys at their lockers. The one who was laughing the loudest earlier was stating how funny the look on Joshua's face was when he read the note.

Anger surged through me, and I stomped up to the boy and shoved him into his locker. He whipped around, confusion clear on his face. I held the wrinkled-up paper in his face and shouted, "You think this is funny? This isn't funny you inconsiderate asshole!"

He placed his hands on my shoulders and moved me backwards, out of his personal bubble. I glared down at one of his hands on my shoulder before lifting the glare up to meet his gaze. "How about you keep your filthy hands off me, Jackass."

A hand gripped my arm, pulling me away from the boy I had just verbally assaulted. I turned my head to see Joshua, who was pulling me away from the boy. "Just let it go, Delta."

I huffed out a breath and walked with him, pulling my arm out of his grasp. "He shouldn't have said that stuff. It's not funny, and it's not okay."

Joshua stuffed his hands in his pockets and said, "Well, technically, he didn't say anything."

I rolled my eyes and shoved him. "You know what I meant."

I stopped at my locker and waved at Joshua as he continued without me to his locker. As I twisted in my combination, someone walked up to me. I recognized him as the boy who wasn't laughing with his friends when they insulted Joshua. I looked him up and down before growling out, "What do you want?"

He had his hands tucked into the pockets of his black hoodie. He had his hood flipped up, covering part way down his forehead. Even with the shadow it cast on his face, I could still see the dark circles under his eyes, and the almost dead look in his eyes. He almost reminded me of Joshua when we were kids. The difference being Joshua was always so full of life.

He cleared his throat, and in a gravelly voice, said, "I just wanted to apologize for my friends. They act like dicks sometimes, but they're really not that bad."

I chuckled dryly. "Yeah, telling someone to kill themselves. They sound like some real standup guys."

I turned to walk away, but he followed. I frowned at him and stopped walking. He turned to face me and continued, "Yeah, I guess saying something shitty like that makes it really hard to believe that they're really not that bad." He looked down at the ground.

"Do you want something else or are you going to start following me again if I walk away?" I asked, impatiently.

"Uh, I just wanted to apologize for them. I wanted to apologize to your boyfriend too, but I guess he already went to class."

I couldn't help but laugh at that assumption. He raised an eyebrow at me as I shook my head. "Sorry, but Joshua is not my boyfriend. He's basically my brother, so that thought...it's ridiculous."

"Oh...sorry for assuming..."

The anger from before was gone now. I noticed how awkward and nervous the boy seemed. I sighed and stuck my hand out for a handshake and said, "I'm Delta."

He looked at my hand before hesitantly taking it in his own. As he gave it a light shake, he said, "I'm Osbourne."

Chapter 2

I was lying on my bed, staring at the ceiling. I kept replaying what had happencd with Osbourne over and over in my head. I couldn't help but wonder why he felt the need to apologize for his friends. He hadn't done anything and hadn't laughed, so why did he apologize? I had been thinking about this since it had happened.

I was pulled out of my thoughts by a pillow landing on my face and someone saying, "Earth to Delta."

I sat up, crossing my legs, and hugging the pillow to my chest. I looked across my room at Joshua and tucked a clump of hair behind my ear. "What's up?"

He raised an eyebrow at me before saying, "I've been talking to you for the past five minutes, but you've been spacing out. Staring at the ceiling."

"Sorry," I mumbled as I fiddled with the pillow.

"Okay," he huffed, standing up and walking over to me. He collapsed, lying on the bed beside me. "What's occupying that pretty little head of yours."

I looked over his face, just taking in his features for a moment. I looked away taking a breath before spilling my thoughts to him. "Okay, so, you know those guys who threw that shitty note at you in English?"

He sighed and sat up. "That's what you're thinking about. Del, you have to let it go."

I cut him off before he could start lecturing me. "No, it's not what you think." I sighed and stood up, pacing for a second before sitting back down. "They had a friend with them. He was really quiet, didn't find what they did funny. Well, after you went off to class, he came up to me and apologized for his friends. He seemed really earnest about it too. I just keep thinking about it."

Joshua looked deep in thought as he said, "Oh."

"Oh?"

"Uh...it's...just not what I expected. I thought you were still pissed."

I scoffed. "Well, I would have every right to be."

"So, who was the friend?" He redirected the subject.

"Uh, Osbourne."

"Osbourne?" He asked while standing up. He walked over to my bookshelf.

I looked at him in confusion and asked, "Uh, whatcha doin?"

"Looking for last year's yearbook," he mumbled as he grabbed a thin book off the shelf. "Here it is."

"Why?" I asked, still confused.

"Because I'm curious who he is, and he may have gone to school with us last year."

"Oh," I said, now understanding.

He began flipping through the pages to find the junior class. Once he found the page he was looking for, he stopped and looked at me. "Do you happen to know his last name?"

I shook my head and said, "No."

"Okay, this will take a little longer then. I'll just have to look through all the names."

"Or you could hand me the book, and I could find his picture."

"That works too," he mumbled as he passed me the book.

I flipped through the pages, searching for the dark-haired boy I had met earlier that day. It wasn't long before I found him. I checked the name to ensure I had the right person. The name read, "Osbourne Jackson." I pointed at his picture and turned the book to Joshua. "This is him."

"Osbourne Jackson," he mumbled. "I don't recognize him. I thought maybe he knew me from a different class or something."

"Well, he wanted to apologize to you too, on behalf of his friends."

Joshua looked up at me. "Really?"

I nodded. "But you'd already gone to class."

Joshua looked deep in thought, and he nodded. He tilted his head to the side and said, "It's a little strange that he apologized."

"That's what I keep thinking about. I thought it was weird that he apologized for his friends."

"Maybe he just didn't want to be associated with that kind of behavior? Or maybe we're thinking too much about it."

"Maybe. Maybe we should just forget about it and move on."

"Sounds like a plan," he said as he nudged my arm.

Chapter 3

As much as I tried to fight it, my thoughts were still focused on the strange apology from the day before. I walked through the day in a haze, and before I knew it, I was half-way through the lunch period with my friends staring at me. I was pulled from the thoughts by a hand waving in front of my face. I swatted the hand away and looked around the table, met with curious faces.

Violet pulled her hand away from me and asked, "You okay, Dee? You've, like, zoned out the entire conversation."

"Uh, yeah. I'm fine. Just have some stuff on my mind." I glanced at Joshua as I said this, and he had a mild look of concern directed at me.

"You sure you're okay?" Joshua asked.

"Uh, yeah," I drew out. "I just keep thinking about what we talked about yesterday."

"Oooo," Marco sounded, suggestively, while waggling his eyebrows and looking between us.

Joshua punched his brother, mumbling at him to shut up. Joshua directed his attention back at me. "Do you wanna open up the discussion to the whole table?"

Before I could respond, Scarlet interjected herself into the conversation. "Well, you don't really have an option now, do you? If you wanted the convo to stay private, should've kept it in the bedroom." Scarlet often insinuated that Joshua and I were secretly sleeping together.

I rolled my eyes and mumbled, "Whatever." I cleared my throat before summarizing the events from the day before in a louder voice.

Scarlet was playing with her salad with her fork, looking uninterested in the conversation. "So, who was the loser who apologized for his friends?"

I looked at Scarlet, and I hesitated to tell her his name. Scarlet tended to be critical of others. For reasons I did not know or understand, I didn't want Scarlet to speak poorly of Osbourne. I took a breath and said, "His name is Osbourne."

Scarlet scoffed, "You don't mean Osbourne Jackson?"

As much as I had wished that she didn't, I wasn't surprised that Scarlet knew who he was. Scarlet knew the names of nearly everyone at school. She always said that knowledge was power, and she believed the more people you knew, the more power you had and more power you had over others.

A sudden nervousness had washed over me, and I hesitantly responded, "Uh, yeah."

Scarlet rolled her eyes, "Of course a dweeb like him would apologize for someone else. Just forget about it, Del. He's a loser, a nobody. He's definitely not worth worrying over."

"How do you know him, Scar?" Joshua cut in.

Scarlet looked up at him and paused. She went back to her salad before continuing. "You guys remember when I lived over in Everett?"

"Yeah, how could we forget that shitty place? We all were worried you'd get shot there," Marco chimed in.

Scarlet nodded, "Yeah, well, Osbourne lived in the same apartment building. As far as I know, he still lives somewhere in Everett. Although, I heard he's living in a house on the better side now. Not that it matters." She set her fork down, now finished with her salad. "He's just a loser who's going nowhere in life. He'll always be stuck in Everett." Before Scarlet could go on anymore, the bell rang, dismissing us from lunch.

I slowly stood up and gathered my trash, intentionally lagging behind everyone else at the table. I continued to drag my feet to throw my trash away and to head to my locker. As I exited the cafeteria, I came face-to-face with Joshua, who had been waiting for me to come out. He bumped my shoulder with his as we walked towards the lockers. "You okay?"

I shrugged and glanced at him. "Scarlet was pretty harsh in there," I mumbled.

He grabbed my arm and pulled me to face him, stopping us from walking farther. "Ignore Scarlet. If you're curious about him, just talk to him."

I pushed his hand away and looked at him with furrowed eyebrows. "I'm not interested in him. I just want to understand why he apologized."

Joshua rolled his eyes. "Yeah, whatever. Just ask him about it. He's in this class with us. Just talk to him."

With that said, Joshua walked away and to his locker, leaving me alone to process what he'd said. I slowly turned and continued on to my locker.

Walking into the classroom and taking my seat beside Joshua, I was still thinking about what Joshua had said. I wasn't sure about talking to Osbourne. I wasn't sure what I would say if I did. I sat and stared at Osbourne. I struggled to focus on the class, and at one point, Osbourne's friends caught me staring. I quickly broke my gaze when they got Osbourne's attention—no doubt informing him of my creepy staring.

I had overthought the entire situation, and I was now desperate to be out of the classroom. I had started tapping my fingers on my desk, and I was bouncing my leg in anticipation of the dismissal bell. I bit the bottom of my lip, hoping I would be fast enough to escape the classroom before anyone could confront me over the staring. I wished I had listened to Scarlet and let it go.

When the bell rang, I was the first one out of the room, even though I was one of the farthest from the door. I made the mistake of thinking that I was in the clear, but I was approached at my locker.

"What do you want with Osbourne?" I glanced at the boy leaning against the locker next to me. He was the boy I had yelled at the day before. He was staring intensely at me with his arms crossed over his chest.

"Excuse me?"

"Look, I know you think I'm an asshole because I hurt your friend's feelings, but don't think about doing anything to Osbourne to get back at me."

I clenched my fists as anger flushed through me. "I wouldn't do something like that, because unlike you, I'm not an asshole." I unintentionally stepped closer to him as I spoke, anger increasing with each word. "I was just curious why he felt the need to apologize for a prick like you."

He placed his hands on my shoulders and moved me backwards, out of his personal space. "You really like invading personal bubbles when you get worked up."

Irritation filling my voice, I snapped, "You done? Can I go now?"

He sighed and pushed off the locker. "Look, Osbourne is a good guy. Don't screw with his head, okay? If you do, I'll make your life hell."

He tried to walk away, but I grabbed his arm and stopped him. "You have some nerve coming up to me with accusations as if I actually did anything to suggest any form of animosity towards your friend. I don't have any problem with Osbourne. You, however...you owe Joshua an apology, Dickhead."

He raised an eyebrow at me and said, "My name isn't 'Dickhead."

"Yeah, well, I don't know what your name is."

"It's Bowie."

"I like 'Dickhead' better."

"Stop calling me 'Dickhead," and I'll apologize to your friend."

"Deal." I held out my hand to seal the agreement with a handshake.

He shook it while saying, "I think it's only fair that you tell me your name now."

"It's Delta."

I looked behind Bowie and saw Joshua approaching us. I looked back at Bowie and smirked. "Now's your chance to apologize. Joshua is walking this way."

He groaned and turned to face Joshua, who was now standing with us by my locker.

Joshua looked at me inquisitively. I smiled smugly and announced, "Joshy, Bowie has something he'd like to say to you."

Bowie snickered, "Joshy?" I punched Bowie in the arm, making him yelp and grab the inflicted area. "Fine. I'm sorry about the note I threw at you yesterday, Josh."

Joshua looked back and forth between us before saying, "That's the first time anyone has ever called me Josh."

Bowie turned to me and whined, "I apologized. We good now?"

Before I could answer, Joshua interrupted. "Delta, why did you make him apologize?"

"Because you deserved an apology."

He rolled his eyes before saying, "I think you know what I'm getting at, but I can spell it out for you. Although, I don't think you really want me to say it in front of him." He motioned to Bowie.

"I think you should spell it out for her," Bowie chimed in.

I looked away from him and mumbled, "I don't know what you're talking about."

He was quiet for a moment before saying, "Okay then. You were supposed to talk to Osbourne since you haven't been able to stop thinking about him and what happened yesterday. You took too long and have overthought the situation and feel embarrassed that you got caught looking at him while debating trying to have a conversation with him."

My cheeks turned red, and I glanced at Bowie, who had the biggest smirk on his face.   "So you were staring at him because you're a stalker with a crush?" He chuckled.

"That is not what he just said," I growled at him.

"Well, the longer you take to just start a conversation with him, the more you seem like a stalker with a crush," Joshua sternly stated.

"Catch him at the end of the day. I'll keep Arvin busy, and you'll be free to talk uninterrupted," Bowie offered.

I looked at him suspiciously. "Why would you offer to help me? We aren't exactly buddies."

He started to walk away but stopped to answer my question. "Well, that may be true, but you're not that bad. I know—I was pretty critical of you to start with, but I see now that you're just defensive of your friends, which I can respect. Osbourne is a good guy, and you shouldn't be afraid to talk to him." He started to walk away again. He stopped to add in one final thought, "But my threat still stands. Don't screw with his head or else I'll make your life a living hell."

After he was out of listening distance, Joshua said, "I didn't expect him to apologize or to be as friendly as he just was. I expected a lot more hostility."

"Yeah...Osbourne did say that his friends weren't all that bad," I mused.

"So," Joshua said and looked at me.

"So?" I asked.

"Sooo, what's the game plan?"

I started walking towards my next class, and Joshua followed. As we walked, I asked, "Game plan for what?"

Joshua scoffed and said, "Seriously? What's the plan for meeting up with Osbourne? What are you going to say?"

I stopped walking, gripping my books tightly against my chest. I said, just above a whisper, "Maybe I shouldn't meet up with him. Maybe this is all just a bad idea."

Joshua rolled his eyes and shoved me. "You're overthinking again." He started walking again, and I followed. "You're going to walk up to him and just say the first thing that comes to mind. Trust your gut."

"Trust my gut?"

"Yeah. It's not like you're crushing on the guy or anything, so there's no need to be so nervous."

I nodded, "You're right. I think I just let Scar get in my head about him."

"That's why you're nervous. You're afraid Scarlet will find out that you want to talk to him, get to know him a little bit. Maybe be friends with him. You worry too much about her disapproval."

"Not everyone can be as carefree as you, Joshie," I smiled and pat his shoulder before parting ways with him to head to my class.

The rest of the day passed quickly, and before I knew it, it was time for me to find Osbourne and attempt a conversation with him. I let out a heavy sigh before making my way through the hallways, looking through the swarms of people for him. It wasn't long before I'd gone through all the halls that I thought he might be in. Feeling defeated, I stepped outside and headed for the parking lot. Looking around at all the cars, I finally spotted him with his friends. I caught Bowie's gaze, and he had a smug look on his face. I almost turned the other direction, worried he was just planning to embarrass me in front of his friends. Before I could, Bowie wrapped his arm around Arvin and directed his attention to some girls who were dressed in clothes that showed a lot of skin. With a deep breath, I quickly walked over to Osbourne, who was paying no attention to his two friends.

I took Joshua's advice and said the first thing that came to mind when I approached Osbourne. "Bowie's kind of a weird guy, isn't he?"

Osbourne looked at me with eyebrows furrowed. He let out a chuckle and said, "Kind of. I didn't think you cared much for him."

"Well, he apologized to Joshua, so I guess he's growing on me."

Osbourne raised an eyebrow at me, "How'd you manage that? Bowie's not a bad guy, but he is stubborn. Getting him to admit he's wrong is like pulling teeth."

I awkwardly smiled and said, "I can be very persuasive."

He laughed and said, "I'm not sure if I wanna know what that means."

I laughed and said, "I guess I'm just a little more stubborn than he is."

We fell into an awkward silence for a moment. Osbourne cleared his throat, breaking the silence, "So did you come all the way over here to tell me that Bowie is weird?"

I looked at the ground, feeling my cheeks warm up. "No," I chuckled. "I wanted to talk to you but didn't know what to say." I looked back up at him. "Joshua told me to trust my gut and say the first thing that came to mind. Last time I take his advice."

Osbourne smiled at me, "I don't know. It was a pretty interesting conversation starter. Broke the ice pretty good."

I smiled back at him, "Yeah, I guess so."

"I do need to go home, but feel free to come tell me how weird Bowie is. Any time."

I laughed and waved as he walked towards a car near where his friends stood. I turned and made my way to where my car was parked with a smile on my face, feeling as though I had accomplished something huge. I didn't know then how much things would change. I wish I could have held on to that moment much longer than I did.

Chapter 4

It was finally the weekend, and I had plans with Violet, Scarlet, Marco, and Joshua. We were going to Mukilteo to walk along the beach. I, like always, was running late. I was rushing around to get ready, and my dad was yelling up the stairs at me to stop stomping. As I ran down the stairs, my dad met me at the bottom, giving me a stern look.

"You sound like krava stampede. Why the stomping?"

I looked at him in confusion and asked, "Otac, what's krava?"

He sighed dramatically and said, disappointedly, "You must study, Nova. Krava is cow. You sound like cow running."

I laughed loudly, "I don't sound like a cow!"

"Da, you stomp, stomp, stomp. Just like running krava."

"Whatever, Otac. I'm running late to meet my friends, and I still have to pick up Joshua and Marco."

"Have fun. Be safe."

"We will!" I yelled back at him as I ran out the front door and to my car.

While the drive to the beach was short, it seemed much longer with Marco complaining the entire time. He didn't think it was fair that Joshua always sat in the front seat, and he made sure to tell us all about how unfair it was. He also complained about me always being late. Joshua and I both sighed in relief when we finally pulled into the parking lot at the beach. We quickly unbuckled our seatbelts and scrambled out of the car. Marco barely got out of the car before I locked the doors. Joshua and I briskly walked away from the car, forcing Marco to jog to catch up to us.

"Now you guys are leaving me behind. You guys are such dicks. I'm practically invisible when it's just the three of us."

"Maybe we would acknowledge you more if you complained less," I suggested.

I quickly scanned the beach for Violet and Scarlet. Marco spotted them first, and Joshua tugged on my sleeve and pointed in the direction they were in. Marco shoved us out of his way as he sprinted towards the girls. I shook my head as I walked behind Joshua in their direction.

"It's about time you three get here," Scarlet snipped.

Marco pointed at me and said, "It's her fault. She's always late."

Scarlet rolled her eyes at me and mumbled, "Slow ass."

I smiled and flipped her off.

The next couple hours were spent filled with laughter, pushing, teasing, and trying to shove Marco into the water. I was laughing at Marco trying—and failing—to pick up Violet so that he could throw her in the water when Joshua nudged me. I looked at him with a big smile stretched across my face, and he pointed in the direction of the parking lot. Bowie, Arvin, and Osbourne were walking this way. Bowie caught my eye, and he gave me a playful smirk while flipping me off. I rolled my eyes and looked away. A sudden nervousness crept through me. I looked back at Marco and Violet. Marco was lying on his belly on the ground, and Violet was sitting on top of him. I chuckled.

"Great," Scarlet growled sarcastically.

I looked up at her, and she was looking in the direction of Osbourne and his friends. The nervousness grew stronger, and I felt nauseous.

"What?" Joshua asked with a knowing look.

"Those losers are really walking over here." Scarlet shook her head in disbelief before scowling at me. "You ignored me and talked to him, didn't you?"

I wiped my sweaty palms on my jeans. "Why does it matter? I can talk to whomever I want."

"Trust me, Del. You do not want to be associated with losers like them."

I stared at her, unsure what to say. The silence was awkward, and the awkwardness only increased when Bowie, Arvin, and Osbourne walked up to us.

"Hey, Delta, Josh." Bowie greeted.

"Hey, Bowie," I replied as Joshua gave a small head nod.

"What do you losers want?" Scarlet snapped.

"Well, we thought we saw a distressed beached whale, but it was just you," Arvin snapped back casually.

As hard as I tried not to, I laughed at the comment. I thought Scarlet was going to kill me with the look she gave me. I quickly cleared my throat and looked down at my feet to hide the smile that was still stretched across my face.

"Look, just because Delta has bad taste, that doesn't mean the rest of this group does. So you should just leave, and maybe take her with you."

My head snapped up, and I glared at Scarlet. "What the hell is that supposed to mean?"

"Can we all just stop fighting?" Violet piped up, still sitting on Marco.

"Oh fuck," Bowie yelled in surprise. "I didn't see her down there."

Scarlet ignored Bowie's comment and answered Violet. "We can stop fighting when Delta decides what kind of people she wants to invest in." She looks back at me. "You can continue spending time with the people you've known forever and care about you, or you can waste your time with losers you don't even know, one of which told your best friend to kill himself."

"Okay, that's enough," Joshua intervened. "Delta can be friends with people you don't like. If she wasn't allowed to talk to anyone you don't like, she wouldn't associate with anyone outside of this little group. Don't punish her because you're an insufferable bitch. We were leaving anyways, so let's just go."

"Fine," Scarlet snapped, stomping towards the parking lot.

We all followed behind her, and I lagged behind everyone else. I looked at the three boys my friend had insulted. I mumbled, "I'm really sorry about her. I'll see you guys around."

I jogged to catch up with Joshua. Marco decided to catch a ride with Scarlet and Violet, leaving Joshua and I alone in my car. Once alone in the car, Joshua asked, "Do you wanna skip eating out with everyone and go somewhere else?"

Fumbling with my keys, I mumbled, "Why would I want to do that?"

"Because Scarlet is being a bitch."

Starting the car, I sighed. "She's just going to keep harassing me about it all day, isn't she?" I looked over at Joshua.

He nodded. After a moment of silent debate, he said, "You know, we could stay here and hang out with Osbourne and his friends after Scarlet leaves."

I chuckled, "She'd be so pissed if she ever found out."

He scoffed and shouted, "Who cares?! She's not the boss of you, and she sure as hell isn't the boss of me. One day, high school and the high school statuses will all be irrelevant. When you look back on this moment, on today, do you want to wonder what would've happened if you hadn't let Scarlet influence your decisions?"

I sighed and turned the car off. "To hell with Scarlet. I wanted to eat on the beach anyways, and she shot that idea down. Let's go get some Ivar's and eat on the beach."

And that's what we did. We walked to Ivar's and ordered fish and chips to-go, and we walked back to the beach. When we got back, I didn't see Osbourne, Bowie, or Arvin, so Joshua and I just sat in the sand with our to-go boxes and started eating in silence.

"Your friend is a peach," a deep voice commented sarcastically from behind me. I looked over my shoulder to see the three boys I hadn't seen when we got back to the beach.

"Yeah, she tends to be a bitch," Joshua commented.

I chuckled before mumbling, "Be nice."

"Why are you so insistent on everyone being nice?" Bowie grumbled.

"Just let it go," Osbourne mumbled before stepping forward and sitting beside me.

"Hey," I greeted awkwardly. I hadn't expected him to sit beside me.

"Hey," he mumbled back.

"Good lord you guys are awkward," Bowie commented.

Joshua stood up and said, "I'm going to get more fish and chips." He looked at Arvin and Bowie and asked, "You guys wanna come?"

Bowie chuckled and nodded, "Sure." As the three of them walked away, Bowie yelled back, "Don't worry, Jack. I'll get something for you."

We sat in a semi-awkward silence while I ate. I paused for a moment and looked at Osbourne. "I'm really sorry about Scarlet. I wish I could say that she's not always like that, but...she's always like that with most people."

Osbourne was silent for a moment before blurting, "Why are you friends with someone like her?"

I looked at him in surprise.

"Sorry," he shook his head and looked out at the water. "That came out wrong. What I meant was, how is someone as nice as you friends with someone as...critical...as her?"

I chuckled at his word choice. "Our whole friend group knows that Scarlet is a bitch, so it's fine if you want to call her that. Scarlet wasn't so intense when we first met her. I guess we've all been friends long enough that we don't wanna bail on each other just because we've changed over the years."

We fell back into silence and looked out over the water. I chewed on my bottom lip, thinking over the things Scarlet said earlier. I sighed and looked at Osbourne. I was surprised that he was staring intently at me. His eyes widened when I caught him, and he quickly looked away as his cheeks turned a bright red color. The corners of my lips quirked up slightly as I held in a laugh. I sighed and cleared my throat, looking back at the water.

"Just because our friends don't get along doesn't mean we can't be friends, right?"

When he didn't reply, I almost stood up and walked away. Just as I was about to, he said, "Right."

I looked at him, and he was looking at me again. I smiled at him, and he smiled back.

"I really hope Bowie is being nice to Joshua," I commented.

He laughed and said, "After you attacked him at his locker, I doubt he'll ever do anything to Joshua again."

I gasped and placed my hand over my chest. "I did not attack him. I yelled at him. There was no attack."

He raised his eyebrow and looked at me with a smirk. "Yelling is a verbal attack."

I rolled my eyes and mumbled, "Whatever."

A while later, Joshua, Bowie, and Arvin finally returned. Bowie brought back food for Osbourne, as promised. We all sat together as Osbourne started to eat. We all sat in a peaceful silence until Bowie decided to drop a handful of sand down the back of my shirt. I gasped and began chasing him around the beach. I almost had Bowie, but he tripped me. I fell on Arvin, and he joined me in chasing Bowie. Bowie complained about the uneven odds, so Joshua joined in. Osbourne sat, eating, and laughing at the four of us running around and tripping each other.

After an hour of running around, we were all worn out. Joshua and Arvin sat beside Osbourne while Bowie and I stood. Without saying a word, I walked towards the water, slipping my shoes off as I walked. I heard Bowie say, "What the hell is she doing?"

Before Joshua could answer, I yelled, "I'm cooling off."

I walked barefoot into the water, pulling my pant legs up. I stood in the wet sand, letting the tide wash over my feet. I smiled down at the cold water, lost in my own world. I'm pulled out of my thoughts when I hear Osbourne yell, "Delta, run!"

I turned around in confusion, but it was too late. Bowie picked me up by my waist and threw me backwards into the water. My scream is quickly muffled as I'm plunged under the icy water. I sit up quickly with a gasp and a shiver. I look up, wide eyed, at Bowie. He's doubled over, laughing. I quickly launch myself upward into his abdomen, knocking him off balance, making him fall into the water with me.

"Shit!" He yelled as he was drenched in the cold water.

I laughed and scrambled to my feet, running away from the soaked Bowie.

"I tried to warn you," Osbourne laughed.

"Maybe warn me sooner next time," I said with a devious smile. I stooped down in front of Osbourne, who was still sitting in the sand, and I tackled him in a wet hug.

"Shit!" He exclaimed as I squeezed him tight.

Joshua and Arvin laughed at his misfortune.

I laughed as I pushed myself up and off him, sitting in front of him. I pushed my wet hair out of my face and smiled at him. He sat up and looked at me, and I said simply, "Motivation to warn me sooner next time."

"What makes you think there will be a next time?" Bowie grumbled, walking up behind me.

I turned and frowned up at him as he stopped to stand next to where I sat. "Do you think we won't all hang out again sometime?"

"What? You want to keep hanging out with a bunch of losers?" He smirked down at me.

I chuckled and shook my head. "Maybe I'll just keep hanging out with Arvin and Osbourne. They're cooler than you."

"Ha! In your face!" Arvin yelled from beside Joshua.

Joshua stood up and said, "As much fun as this has been, we need to get going. The sun's starting to set."

I looked out over the water behind me, seeing the horizon filled with beautiful reds and oranges as the sun set. "Yeah, we need to get you home."

"What? Is sunset Josh's bedtime?" Bowie teascd.

"My parents don't like me and my brother being out after dark. It's just easier to be home on time," Joshua mumbled.

Joshua and Marco's parents were control freaks, and their mom was paranoid. She insisted that car accidents were more likely to occur at night. She was convinced that if the boys were out after dark, they would be in a car accident.

"See you guys at school," I shouted at them as Joshua and I began walking towards the parking lot.

Chapter 5

M onday rolled around, and I was nervous. Scarlet and I hadn't spoken since the incident at the beach. I wasn't sure what to expect at lunch, and the uncertainty had me anxious all morning. Violet tried reassuring me throughout the day that it would all be fine, but I couldn't shake the feeling that things were about to get worse.

Walking into the lunch room, I took a deep breath to try to ease my nerves. As I approached the table my friends sat at, I knew Scarlet was still pissed. One look at her was enough for anyone to know. Before I could sit down, Scarlet said, "You actually want to sit with us? You don't want to sit with the freaks you traded us in for this weekend?"

Setting the bag that contained my lunch on the table, I looked at Scarlet. "I didn't trade you guys in. I don't see why you care so much about who I spend my time with. I nerve said that you have to like them or hang out with them."

"Well, I don't want to sit with you if you're going to hang out with them. You're a loser by association."

"So you won't be my friend anymore just because I talk to someone you don't like?"

"Look, just say 'thank you' and sit your ass down. I'm doing this to protect you."

"I don't need anyone to protect me. I'm capable of making my own decisions."

"Then you need to decide if you want to forget the losers and sit with us, or maybe you should just sit with them at lunch from now on."

I glanced around the table at my friends, wondering why none of them were willing to defend me. I looked at Marco, who stared down at his tray of food, refusing to look up at me or Scarlet. My gaze moved on to Violet who looked at me in pity and mouthed "sorry" at me. Joshua was the only one missing from the table, and I knew he would have defended me. In that moment, I felt alone. I thought my friends would have my back through anything, but they were too afraid to stand up to Scarlet to defend me. A sad sigh left my lips as I picked up my lunch bag and silently walked away from the table.

Even though I felt crushed that my friends weren't as loyal as I had once thought, I didn't regret my decision to defend Osbourne and his friends. My mom had taught me that we should always be kind to others. You never know what hidden struggles a person might have, and you wouldn't want to be what sends someone over the edge. I knew in my heart that I had made the right decision.

Taking a deep breath, I walked up to the table where Osbourne, Arvin, and Bowie were sitting. Stopping at the end of their table, they all turned to look at me.

"Uhh..." I hesitated. "Can—can I sit with you guys?"

Bowie looked at me, then turned to look in the direction my friends were sitting. Bowie looked back at me and said, "Scarlet's still pissed that you talk to us?"

"She told me that if I'm nice to you guys then I can't sit with her," I mumbled, trying to push away the urge to cry.

Osbourne scooted down on the bench and pat the spot he had been sitting in. "Have a seat."

Bowie groaned. "We're really just letting her join us everywhere now."

I hesitated to sit down. I mumbled, "If it's a problem, I can sit somewhere else."

Osbourne was quick to say, "No, sit! Bowie complains about everything. He wasn't being serious."

"Shit," Bowie said, looking at me. "You look like you're about to cry. Usually, you snap back at me. I didn't think you were a sensitive girl."

I slid into the seat beside Osbourne. Taking a shaky breath, I tried to swallow the emotions rising up. "I just was told that I can't sit with my closest friends that I've had almost my entire life, and none of the others defended me. They just sat there trying to stay on Scarlet's good side. It's a sucky feeling realizing your friends don't have your back as much as you thought."

"Josh didn't say anything to her? He didn't seem worried about what she thought yesterday," Bowie said.

I sighed and sat up, propping my head up with my hand. "Joshua wasn't sitting at the table. I don't know where he is right now."

"So at least you have one friend who'll have your back no matter what. As long as you have one, you aren't completely alone," Arvin commented.

I gave him a small smile. "You're right."

"You can sit with us whenever you want," Osbourne offered.

I smiled at him, "Thanks."

"There's a smile. Good. No more sad bitch." Bowie clapped at me with a smirk stretched across his face. I rolled my eyes while flipping him off and chuckling.

The rest of lunch was spent with laughter and teasing while we ate. I had played out all sorts of scenarios of how lunch would go today, but I never imagined it would turn out the way that it did. At the start of the lunch period, I felt alone. By the end of it, I felt like I had three new friends. I left the lunch room with a smile on my face, telling the boys that I'd see them in English.

As I approached my locker, I saw Joshua leaning against it, waiting for me. "Hey," I greeted him.

"So, you're spending lunch with Osbourne now?" He teased with a smirk.

I cleared my throat and asked, "Scarlet didn't tell you what happened at lunch?"

His eyebrows scrunched together as he looked intently at my face. "What are you talking about?"

I dug through my locker, looking for my English book and notebook. I avoided his gaze when I answered, "We got in an argument. Scarlet doesn't want we sitting with the group if I'm gonna talk to Osbourne, Bowie, and Arvin."

"What did Marco and Violet say about it?"

I chuckled dryly. "They didn't say anything."

"I'm sorry, Del. If I'd been there, I would've told Scarlet to screw off."

I gave him a side hug as we started walking towards the English classroom. "I know you would have, and I appreciate it."

As we slid into our seats, Joshua turned to face me. "Sooo?"

I looked at him in confusion. "So what?"

"So how was lunch with Osbourne?"

"You mean 'lunch with Osbourne, Arvin, and Bowie,' and it was fun."

"You joining us for lunch tomorrow, Josh?" Bowie asked loudly while sliding in the seat in front of me.

"Ooo I get an invite?" Joshua asked.

"Yeah," Arvin began as he took the seat in front of Bowie. "We figured you wouldn't sit with Scarlet without Delta."

"If Delta sits with you guys tomorrow, I will," Joshua answered while watching Osbourne take the seat in front of him.

Looking at the boys around me, it was strange to think how quickly we all became friends. I had plenty of acquaintances, but it had been years since I last made a real friend. When Bowie threw that note at Joshua, I never expected Joshua and I would befriend him, Arvin, and Osbourne. And we never would have if Osbourne hadn't apologized for Bowie.

I looked over at Osbourne with a small smile on my face. It was strange to think something as small as an apology could change so much. He caught my gaze and smiled back at me.

Look back at everything, I wish I'd held on to that moment longer.

Chapter 6

It had been two months since Scarlet and I fought, and Joshua and I had sat with Osbourne, Arvin, and Bowie every day since. Violet still sat with me in class, but she always left first. She didn't talk to me in the hallways anymore, and she only hung out with me if she knew Scarlet wouldn't find out. Marco only spoke to me when I was with Joshua. Neither of them wanted to lose any friends, and they both knew I wouldn't make them choose like Scarlet would. But I was okay with it. I have new friends who accepted me no matter who I spoke to or hung out with. I have friends who didn't make me nervous that they might reject me if I said or did something they didn't approve of.

Over the past two months, Joshua and I had started spending more and more time with Osbourne, Arvin, and Bowie outside of school. There were days when the others were too busy to hang out, so Osbourne and I would have our own little adventures together. Today was one of those days. We were sitting on the beach, watching the calm ocean waves.

I couldn't help but smile when I looked at him. He had changed me so much in the short time I had known him. I felt so free with him. Welcoming me into his group of friends changed my life. I hadn't realized how constricting my group of friends had been with Scarlet dictating our every move until I was away from it.

I looked at him, and a warmth filled my chest. I never would have thought that he and I would ever speak to each other, let alone become close friends, as we had over the past couple months. I silently studied his face. He frowned at me as he caught my gaze on him.

"What?" he chuckled.

I shook my head and laughed, "It's nothing." I looked up at him. I looked into his beautiful blue eyes. "I was just thinking about how much has changed between us."

He nodded and looked out towards the ocean. "I never thought someone like you would notice someone like me." He laughed dryly, "At least not in a good way."

I tucked some hair behind my ear. "I'm not the same person as I was then. I like the version of myself with you much more."

He looked back to me. He searched my eyes with furrowed brows. For what he was searching, I didn't know, but the intensity of his gaze made my heart beat faster. I wanted to look down, away from the heat of his gaze, but I couldn't. I couldn't break away. He leaned closer to me. I felt his breath fan out across my lips. My eyes fluttered closed, and I leaned in closer to him. The side of his nose brushed against mine, and his breath mingled with mine. My heart was beating even faster now. His lips barely grazed my lips, and I felt as though I were trapped in a dream. His fingertips brushed against my cheek, and he tangled his fingers in my hair, pulling me closer. His lips pressed against mine. I wrapped my arms around his neck and pulled him into me, kissing him back. I couldn't imagine a more perfect moment.

Unfortunately our perfect moment was ruined when his phone started ringing. He pulled away and slid his phone out of his pocket, and I read the name that was across the screen: Bowie. I shook my head as Osbourne stood up, answering the call. Of course Bowie would find a way to ruin a moment without actually being here.

While Osbourne and I grew closer over the past couple months, Bowie and I bickered more. While I did consider him a friend, he and I often butted heads. Joshua and Arvin agreed that Bowie and I were more like frenemies. Some days, it seemed like Bowie just tolerated me.

Osbourne hung up with Bowie and walked back over to where I sat beside me with a serious look on his face as he looked out over the water. I slid my hand in his and intertwined my fingers with his.

"Ozzy, is everything okay?" I asked gently.

"Bowie is pretty upset and wants to hang out."

"Well, I suppose we should go get him then." I sighed as I stood up and brushed the sand off the back of my jeans.

Osbourne stood up beside me, brushing the sand off himself. "I'm sorry about our...uh...moment getting interrupted," he apologized trying to avoid eye contact with me. I smiled when I noticed his cheeks turning red.

I grabbed his hand, leading the way back to his car, and said, "It's okay. We'll have plenty of time for more moments." I should have held on tighter to that moment.

The drive to Bowie's house was brief, and he was sat on the porch, waiting. As soon as he saw Osbourne's car, he stood up and briskly walked over. I climbed over the console and fell into the backseat. As Bowie slid into the passenger seat, he looked harshly at me then at Osbourne. "I seriously can't have one fucking moment with you without her around?" He snapped.

I didn't expect the comment to hurt as much as it did. I bit my lip to push away the tears that threatened to spill. Taking a deep breath, I leaned forward and as close as I could to Osbourne while staying as far away from Bowie as I could. I whispered to him, "You can just drop me off at my place."

He nodded, glancing at me in the rearview mirror. He stayed quiet, and I leaned back in my seat, looking out the window. The ride to my house was awkward. As Osbourne slowed to pull into the driveway, Bowie looked around in confusion. "Where the hell are we?"

As Osbourne parked in the driveway, I hopped out of the car as quickly as I could while mumbling, "Thanks." I practically sprinted into the house without looking back. Once I was safe in the confines of my home, tears began spilling down my cheeks. I hated tense situations, and for whatever reason, Bowie scared me whenever he was mad. I'd never had his anger directed at me before, and having him snap at me like he had, I couldn't stop the tears now that I was alone.

My mom had heard me crying and came rushing over to me, pulling me away from the front door that I'd been leaning on and into a side hug as she led me into the kitchen. "Delta, sweetheart, what's wrong?"

"Nothing, Mom. I'm okay."

"Did something happen between you and Osbourne?"

I shook my head. "No, nothing happened with us. Well, actually something did happen, but that's not why I'm crying."

She grabbed my shoulders and turned me to face her. "What happened with you and Osbourne?"

"We kissed," I said as I wiped the tears off my face.

"How was it?"

I sniffled. "It was amazing."

"Awww, the two of you are so cute."

I stood there awkwardly, looking down at my shoes. "Thanks, I guess."

"If things are good—really good—with Ozzy, then why are you crying?"

"Bowie," I mumbled.

My mom sighed heavily and grumbled, "What did he do this time?"

My head shot up, and I frowned at her. "What do you mean 'This time'?"

"Most of the time anymore, if you're upset, it's because Bowie did something."

I shook my head and looked back down at my shoes. "He's just having a bad day and needed time alone with Osbourne."

"And how did he express that need?"

I sighed and looked at my mom, "He yelled."

"He yelled at you?" she asked, surprised.

"Well, not at me. It was directed at Osbourne, but it was about me. He was mad that I was there." I took a deep breath before continuing. "He was mad that I'm always around Osbourne. He just wanted some time alone with his best friend. I can understand why he was upset. It just scared me how mad he was and him being mad at me. It's really not a big deal, and the more I talk about it, the stupider I feel for getting upset. He's probably more mad about whatever it is he's going through today and just got irritated that he couldn't vent to his best friend like he wanted to because I was there."

"Do you feel better now?" My mom asked, pulling me in a hug.

I hugged her back and mumbled, "A little bit."

"What would make it a lot a bit?"

I chuckled and buried my face into her shoulder. I mumbled into her shoulder, "Cookies."

She laughed and pulled away. "Cookies it is."

Making cookies with my mom always made me feel better, and today was no different. We had made homemade chocolate chips cookies and were waiting for them to cool. I always wanted to shove them in my mouth and let my eyes water as they burned my mouth, but my mom would swat my hand when I would try and tell me to stop being such a masochist. She leaned against the counter, guarding the cookies from me, and I sat on the island across from her, staring longingly at the cookies. Our attention was pulled away at the sound of the doorbell.

She turned around and peeked out the window to see who was at the door. She sighed and walked out of the kitchen. I walked over to the cookies while I listened to her opening the door. Suddenly, she yells, "Delta, don't you touch those cookies."

I sighed and walked out of the kitchen to ask her how she knew I was getting into the cookies. As I exited the kitchen, I heard her say, "You must be Bowie."

I froze where I stood, trying to see around my mom, to see if Bowie really was at my house. Before I could see him, I heard him reply, "Uh, yeah. Would it be okay if I talked to Delta alone?"

"Sure, but it'd be a good idea to go somewhere else to talk. Her father will be home from work soon, and he's nosey."

I walked up behind my mom, leaning around her to see Bowie standing in the doorway. I hesitantly said in a quiet voice, "What are you doing here?"

He rubbed the back of his neck and said, "I was hoping we could talk."

My mom stepped away, leaving me unshielded to Bowie and nervousness crept over me. "Why do you want to talk to me?"

"Can't you just come with me and find out? Your mom said it would be better if we talked somewhere else."

Before I could answer, my mom returned with two baggies, each filled with cookies. She handed us each a bag before ushering us out the door and telling us to have fun. We awkwardly stood on the front porch looking at the bags of cookies.

"Does your mom always hand out bags of cookies before making you leave with people you clearly don't want to be alone with?"

"Nope, you're just special," I mumbled while walking away from the front door and toward his car.

Bowie took me to the beach that I'd been at earlier with Osbourne. The drive had been silent, and now, we were sitting in the sand in silence. I opened my bag of cookies and started nibbling on one. I glanced over at Bowie when I heard his baggie opening. He pulled a cookie out and took a big bite out of it.

"These cookies are really good," he muttered.

"Thanks. My mom and I always bake cookies together whenever I'm upset."

He turned to me, and I turned away. "You made these?"

"Yeah, with my mom."

We fell back into an awkward silence. After eating three cookies, I turned to him and blurted, "Why did you come to my house?"

He didn't answer for a moment. Just when I was considering standing up and walking away, he spoke. "After dropping you off, Jack chewed me out about what I said about you always being around."

"So, you wanted to talk to me because Ozzy told you to?"

"No. He doesn't know I'm talking to you."

More silence.

"Okay, if you want to talk to me, you need to start talking, or I'm going back home."

"Yeah, I'm just not the greatest at apologies. I...I don't know where to start."

I chuckled. "You don't have to say anything elaborate. Just say, 'I'm sorry,' and I'll say, 'It's okay.' That's it."

His lips twitched up into a small smile. "It's really easy to make up with you."

I smiled and said, "My parents always say that there's too much ugly in the world. There's no need to add anymore by being petty or cynical."

He nodded and looked down at his hands. "Your parents sound wise."

"They can be."

"You get along with them?"

"Yeah. I know that no matter what happens, I'll always have them. No matter how bad things get, they'll always be there for me."

"That must be nice," he murmured.

"Are your parents the reason you were so upset today?" I asked cautiously.

"My mom let her new boyfriend move in even though she's only known him a month. She has terrible taste in men."

"I'm sorry. That must be very frustrating."

"It is, and I took it out on you today. I—I'm sorry for that."

"Don't worry about it. I got cookies out of it."

He laughed and said, "If we get cookies every time I make you upset, I'll have to do it more often."

I shoved him and said, "That is not nice. If you want cookies, just ask my mom for some. She'll gladly make you cookies."

"If I come over when I'm mad at my mom, will your mom make me cookies?"

"She won't make them for you. She'll make you help her make them."

"Maybe you can just make them with her, and I'll just show up to eat them."

"Nope. If you want the emotional support cookies, you have to put in the effort to make them."

He laughed. "Emotional support cookies?"

"Yeah, they're cookies specifically for emotional crises."

He shook his head as his laughter died down. "You're so weird."

"And you're much happier than you were at the start of the day, all thanks to my weirdness."

"Whatever," he chuckled while standing up and holding his hand out to me. "Let's get you home, Weirdo."

I grabbed his hand and let him pull me to my feet. "You do feel better now, right?" I commented while trying to keep up with his quick pace.

"Yeah, the cookies healed me with their emotional support," he teased, smirking at me while he unlocked the car doors.

I rolled my eyes and mumbled, "Ass."

Chapter 7

It had been a few days since Osbourne and I kissed, and I shared cookies with Bowie. Osbourne and I hadn't spoken about the kiss, but Bowie kept discreetly slipping me notes asking for more cookies. I told Bowie to go screw himself several times, but he continued to ask for cookies. The day was almost over. Only one class left, but unfortunately, I shared that class with Bowie. Of course, he slid into the seat next to me.

"Hey, Dee, when are you bringing me cookies?"

"Hey, Bowie, when are you shutting the hell up about the cookies?"

"You know, I'll stop asking if you just bring them."

"Maybe I have more important things to worry about than making you some damn cookies," I grumbled as I doodled angrily in my notebook.

"Are you and Jack fighting or something?"

I looked up at him, furrowing my eyebrows. "No. Why would you think we're fighting?"

"Because you're being all moody. I figured it had something to do with him. Especially since you've been staring at him a lot more lately and not talking to him as much."

My cheeks warmed as color flushed them. "I haven't been staring at him," I squeaked.

He rolled his eyes and said, "I'd call you a stalker if I didn't know he's just as obsessed with you as you are with him."

"He has a funny way of showing it," I mumbled.

"Okay, spill," he said, turning in his desk to face me. "What's going on with you two?"

"Why do you want to know so bad?"

"If I help you with this, you'll owe me. By that, I mean you'll owe me some fucking cookies. Now, spill. What's going on?"

I reluctantly said, "The day my mom and I made those cookies, Osbourne and I kissed."

"Okay...what's the big deal? You both clearly like each other. This is a good thing. It's progress."

"Yeah, it was great, but we haven't talked about it since it happened. Things feel more awkward and weird every day that we don't talk about it. I don't know if he regrets it, and it kind of feels like he's avoiding me."

"He's probably just nervous. Maybe he thinks you'd rather forget about it."

"Why would he think that?"

"Have you tried talking to him about the kiss?"

"Well, no."

"He might think you don't want to talk about it then. Maybe he's worried you changed your mind about things after I was all pissy that day."

I smirked at him and teased, "So you're saying it's all your fault then?"

He smirked and shook his head. "What I'm saying is that maybe you should make a move. Invite him out somewhere. Do something to show him that you're still interested."

I scrunched up my nose and asked, "Like what?"   "I don't know. Take him out, take him dancing. I'm not good with romantic shit."

I chuckled. "You think I should take your best friend dancing?"

"Maybe. Seems like something he'd like."

I took Bowie's advice. I texted Osbourne, telling him to meet me at the beach at 7. He hadn't texted back, so I sat nervously in the sand. I looked out over the water, watching the waves wash up over the sand, over the shells lying in the sand. The wind ruffled my hair around. I tried to push it back, out of my face. I jumped when a familiar voice said, "Maybe you should try a hair tie." He laughed when I gasped.

He sat beside me and said, "Sorry. I didn't mean to scare you."

I smiled at him and said, "It's okay."

"So...what did you want to meet about?"

"Maybe I just wanted to hang out."

"Is that it?"

I smiled and shook my head. "I wanted to talk to you."

"Talk away."

"Things have been weird with us lately."

"Have they?" He asked.

I turned to him, looking over his face inquisitively. "Haven't you noticed? Or were you too busy avoiding me to notice?"

He sucked in a breath. "You noticed that?"

I scoffed. "Of course I noticed. I just don't know why."

"Because I was putting off you telling me that you just want to stay friends."

I looked at him intently for a moment before asking, "Who said that that's what I wanted?"

He shrugged and said, "Nobody said it. It's just what I've been expecting. Isn't that why you wanted me to meet you here today?"

"No."

"Then why?"

I stood up, pulling out my phone, and said, "Stand up."

"What?"

"Just stand up."

He stood up, and I pressed play on my Spotify playlist I prepared for this.

"Dance with me," I demanded.

"You told me to meet you so that I would dance with you on the beach," he asked in confusion.

"Yes, now dance with me," I said seriously.

He smiled and pulled me to him. We danced slowly. He held me close, and he rested his forehead against mine. My eyelids fell closed, and I wished I could live in that moment forever. There was a sick feeling in my stomach, and I couldn't shake the thought that we wouldn't be together like this much longer. The thought made my chest feel tight, and tears quickly formed in my eyes. I quickly forced the thought away and focused on the moment. I didn't know what was to come, but I wanted to enjoy the moment. He was there with me, and that's all I cared about. I had him in my arms, and he had me in his.

He whispered in my ear, "Why the sudden need to dance with me?"

"I didn't know what to do to fix things, and Bowie annoyed me into talking to him about what's been going on. I'm just following his advice."

He chuckled and asked, "Bowie told you to dance with me on the beach?"

"He told me to take you dancing. The beach was my idea."

"And why the beach?" he asked, pulling away enough to look me in the eyes.

"Because this is where we kissed," I answered as my heartbeat sped up.

He smiled at me, bringing his face closer to mine. His nose brushed mine, and his breath fanned out across my lips. My eyelids closed, and my breath caught in my throat. His palm rested against my cheek, and we stopped dancing. His lips barely brushed mine, and I felt as though I were on fire. I rested my hand on his chest before grabbing his shirt and pulling him into me, pressing my lips against his. He kissed me back, holding me close to him. My heart raced, and in that moment, I felt complete. It wasn't long before he pulled away from the kiss, both of us breathing heavily. He rested his forehead against mine and smiled down at me.

"I'm really glad you invited me dancing."

I laughed. "I definitely owe Bowie some cookies."

He looked at me with his eyebrows drawn together and laughed, "What?"

I smiled and wrapped my arms around his neck. "It's nothing. Don't worry about it."

He smiled back and wrapped his arms around my waist and said, "If you say so."

We stayed on the beach until after dark. We stared up into the dark sky, looking at the stars and pointing out constellations. I couldn't have dreamed of a more perfect night. If only things could have always been that perfect.

Chapter 8

Since things had gone so well with Osbourne, I surprised Bowie with cookies. Arvin was not happy that Bowie got cookies and he didn't. Bowie was happy to rub it in that he had cookies and no one else did.

"I still don't understand why you had to make him cookies," Osbourne whispered to me at lunch.

"Because I owed him," I whispered back.

"But why?"

"Just because."

"You know, there are other people sitting here and can hear you," Joshua whispered to us.

I looked up at him then over to Arvin and Bowie. All of them were staring at us.

"Did Bowie blackmail you for cookies?" Arvin asked.

"That's exactly what I did," Bowie interjected.

"I don't think it was blackmail," Osbourne began. "At the beach last night, you said that you owed him cookies now," he continued, directing his attention to me.

"Ooo what were you two doing at the beach?" Joshua asked, wiggling his eyebrows at me.

"Who cares about the beach?!" Arvin shouted while standing up, slamming his hands on the table. "I want cookies too."

I stared at him with wide eyes. "I never knew you were so serious about cookies."

Before the cookie discussion could commence any further, the bell rang, signaling the end of lunch. After going our separate ways to our lockers, we all met back in the English classroom. Bowie complained about Osbourne stealing his seat when Osbourne sat at the desk in front of mine.

"Come on, Bowie. He just wants to sit with his girlfriend," Joshua teased, smirking at Osbourne and me. I looked at Osbourne, and I was certain that my face was just as red as his.

Osbourne cleared his throat and said, "Well, technically she's not my girlfriend."

Bowie laughed loudly and yelled, "Oh damn! You just messed up," and high-fived Arvin.

Osbourne quickly looked at me and stammered, "We just haven't talked about it. I mean, I haven't officially asked you or anything."

I leaned forward, placed my hand on his shoulder, and said, "It's okay, Ozzy. You really don't need to explain. We'll figure this," I motioned between us, "out on our own time. Don't let those girlfriend-less dorks pressure you into rushing anything."

"Hey!" Joshua and Arvin exclaimed at the same time.

Bowie scoffed and said, "Why do you assume that I don't have a girlfriend?"

"Because I've heard you talk," I said flatly.

Osbourne and Arvin laughed.

Bowie rolled his eyes and mumbled, "Whatever."

"Hey, do you guys wanna go for ice cream after school?" Arvin asked.

"Sure," I agreed loudly while the rest of our group mumbled responses and grunts of agreement.

After school, as agreed, we all went to Cold Stone Creamery. While Arvin, Bowie, and Osbourne argued about which ice cream flavor was best, Joshua pulled me to the side so that we could talk alone.

"So, how are things going with Osbourne?"

I glanced over at Ozzy and smiled when he flipped off Bowie over a comment about brownies being for bitches. I looked back at Joshua and said, "I really like him. He makes everything better."

"I was worried that you'd start overthinking about things after what happened in English."

"Oddly enough, Ozzy overthinks more than I do. I think things will be okay, and it'll all work out."

"I'm glad to hear that. You seem a lot happier with him around."

I looked at my shoes and smiled before looking back up and smiling at Joshua. "I am a lot happier with him around." I paused and looked over at Osbourne, Arvin, and Bowie. "It's not just him, though. It's all three of them. I've always loved you, Marco, Violet, and Scarlet, but being friends with them is different."

He nodded and said, "I know what you mean. I think it has been good for us both, branching out to a new friend group."

I smiled and slid my arm around his waist, and he wrapped his arm around my shoulders. I sighed contently and said, "I think you're right."

Just as we all received the ice cream we had ordered, Scarlet, Violet, and Marco walked in. I huffed and mumbled, "Great."

Bowie, who had been standing behind me, leaned over my shoulder and whispered, "She must be here for the brownies."

As hard as I tried, I couldn't hold back the laugh that escaped at that comment. I turned around and smacked him while everyone turned to look at me, including the three people who had just walked in.

"Ew," Scarlet commented when her gaze fell on me.

I rolled my eyes. "Don't worry, Brownie Lover. We're leaving," I said as I led the boys outside.

"Where we going?" Arvin asked, looking more interested in his ice cream than the answer to his question.

"I don't know," I shrugged. "I just didn't want to be in there with Scarlet, and I figured none of you wanted to be either."

"Yeah, I don't feel like being called a worthless loser today," Arvin commented casually.

"Why'd you call her a 'Brownie Lover'?" Joshua asked.

"Because Bowie said that brownies are for bitches," I chuckled. The boys laughed.

We just walked around, aimlessly. We teased and shoved each other around, and we laughed. We had fun just being with each other. I would give anything to be able to live in moments like that. To live in the happy moments. I was so carefree and enjoyed life, blissfully unaware of what was coming.

Chapter 9

The worst day of my life was a Saturday. It started like any other Saturday. I woke up late, and I knew my parents had already left. They always did the shopping on the weekends. It was their thing. They even went when the weather was bad. Bad like it was on that Saturday. They should've stayed home with it raining as hard as it was, but they never let the rain stop them. My dad would always say that it was no worse than the rain in Serbia. That was always his justification for things here. It would be okay because it was no worse than the way things were when he lived in Serbia. I wished he had been a little more cautious or worried.

One phone call. That's all it took to change my life forever. One phone call to tear down my life as I knew it. Just one phone call to set me on a course for more heartbreak than I ever thought was possible and was so sure I would never survive. I never thought that a phone call could hurt me. But that call...that one call...it was enough to make me feel as though I would never breathe again.

I was tucked sloppily in bed with some stupid movie on when the call came. I didn't check who was calling, assuming it was either Joshua or Osbourne. The unfamiliar voice that came through startled me when it asked, "Is this Delta Novak?"

I hesitantly replied, "Uh, yes, this is she. What's this about?"

"I work for Overlake Medical Center. I just need to clarify: Your parents are Nikita and Lillian Novak?"

A heaviness settled in my chest, and I felt strangled. "Yes, those are my parents. Why are you asking if they're my parents?"

"I'm sorry to inform you, but your parents were in an accident. You were the only one they had listed as an emergency contact, apart from each other."

"Are...are they going to be okay?" Tears began flowing down my cheeks.

"They're in surgery now, but they are in critical condition."

"No," I whimpered and began sobbing. I took a breath and asked, "You said Overlake Medical?"

"Yes, Ma'am."

"Is there anything else you can tell me right now?"

"Not at this time."

"Thank you," I mumbled and hung up.

With shaking hands, I fumbled through my contacts on my phone and clicked on "Joshua." Choking on sobs, I waited for him to answer. Panic coursed through me when he didn't answer. I knew I was in no condition to drive myself. I tried calling Marco, Violet, and Scarlet. No one answered. I tried calling Osbourne, and he didn't answer either. Tears poured down my face, and the sobs were suffocating. My thumb hovered over one last name. The name of someone

I least expected to answer. After three rings, his voice came through clear and teasing, "Get bored with Jack already?"

With a shaky voice, I whimpered, "Bowie?"

"Whoa, are you crying? Please don't tell me you guys split. I'll feel like such an asshole."

"Bowie," I breathed, trying to calm myself enough to speak. "I-I need help. I need...I need a ride. No one will answer their damn phones. You're the only one." Another sob broke through.

"Text me the address of wherever you are. I'll leave now."

It was ten minutes after I texted him the address when I heard a knock on the door. To me, it felt like an eternity.

I opened the door, knowing I was a mess, and with a strangled breath, I wrapped my arms around him. He held me and rubbed my back. "What's going on?" he whispered to me.

"I need a ride to the hospital," I whimpered.

He pulled away and looked me over. "Are you okay?"

I nodded and said, "It's my parents. There was an accident."

He looked me in the eyes. "Oh shit. Yeah, let's get going. I'm sure you're freaking out. Which hospital?"

"Overlake Medical."

Bowie drove like hell, and it didn't take long for us to pull up to the hospital. There was still nothing new that they could tell me, and I was directed to the waiting room. Bowie stayed with me, and I was thankful. I didn't want to drown in all of this alone.

"I was really the only person who answered?" Bowie broke the silence.

I had finally stopped crying, and I felt numb. My voice was scratchy when I answered, "Yeah. I called Joshua, Marco, Violet, Scarlet, and Osbourne. When I called you, you were the one I least expected to answer. Funny how things work out like that."

"I'm surprised Jack didn't answer."

I glanced at Bowie. "Why do you call him that? Jack?"

"Because his last name is Jackson, and he prefers when I call him that than when I call him OJ."

I chuckled. "You seriously call him OJ?"

He smirked and said, "Not anymore."

"It's strange to just call him by part of his last name."

"What's your last name?"

I looked at him in confusion and answered, "Novak?"

"You say it like you're not sure that's your last name."

"No, it's my last name. I'm just not sure why you're asking me."

"Okay, Novak. Nobody has ever called you Nova?"

I smiled sadly and looked at my hands. "My dad calls me Nova sometimes. He says it's because I'm explosive and beautiful like a star."

We sat in silence for a moment before Bowie said, "So if you were a superhero, your hero name would be Super Nova?"

I chuckled and mumbled, "I guess." I cleared my throat and said, "Bowie, I'm really glad you're here with me. I...I don't know what I'd do if I were here alone. I know I'd be more of a mess than I am right now."

He looked at me with a sad expression. "Anytime."

I looked at him silently for a moment before saying, "You think I'm going to have to sit in a hospital waiting room like this more than once?"

He chuckled, shook his head, and leaned back in his chair. "That's not what I meant." He hesitated before continuing, "What I meant...I know I'm not your closest friend and the last person you want to rely on, but anytime you feel stuck or like you don't have anyone, you can call me."

An overwhelming amount of emotion washed over me, and in the quietest voice, I squeaked out, "Thank you."

"I mean it." He paused before adding, "Even if things don't work out with you and Osbourne. I know when everything started, I was pretty harsh about if things end badly with you and Osbourne. I don't care if they end badly. If you're in a bad place and need someone, you can call me."

Silent tears ran down my face. I nudged him and whispered, "You're getting soft on me."

He chuckled. "I didn't expect the kind of person you turned out to be. I guess I fucked up and got attached."

I gave him a small smile, but our moment was interrupted by a doctor approaching. We both look up at him, and he asks, "Are you Delta Novak?"

I stood and shakily said, "Yes." I felt sick and a feeling of dread flowed through me. The expression on his face said it all, and tears began flowing down my face. When the words left his lips, it all became too real. I fell to my knees, and my heart shattered. My parents were gone, and the pain I felt was overwhelming. My chest was tight, and I felt as if I were suffocating. A single sentence changed my entire life, and I wished more than anything that I was just having a terrible nightmare. I wished I could wake up and hold my parents. But it wasn't a nightmare. They were gone, and there was nothing I could do to change that.

The doctor gave his condolences and walked away. I remained on the floor, sobbing. Bowie crouched next to me and wrapped his arm around my shoulders. He leaned close to me and whispered, "I'm so sorry, Delta." There was so much emotion in his voice, you would have thought he was the one who lost someone.

I turned to him and wrapped my arms around his neck, and I buried my face in his shoulder and sobbed harder. He wrapped his other arm around me, pulled me closer, and rubbed my back in an attempt to sooth me. We sat there, with the only sound being my sobs, for what felt like an eternity. I pulled away from him and wiped my face on my sleeves. With a shaky breath, I looked at him and croaked out, "I don't know what to do."

He pushed my hair out of my face and said, "I'll take you anywhere you wanna go."

"I don't...I don't know where to go. Just not home."

He nodded and looked in thought. "I know a place."

He stood up, held my hands, and pulled me to my feet. He slid his arm around my shoulders and guided me towards the doors to leave the hospital. I leaned into him, feeling weak and exhausted. It wasn't long before we were in his car and flying down the highway.

We were silent from the moment we left the hospital. I still had that suffocating feeling in my chest, and I couldn't focus on my surroundings. I leaned my head against the window, and I mumbled, "None of this feels real."

Bowie glanced over at me before returning his attention back to the road. He alternated glances between me and the road. He took me by surprise when he reached over and grabbed my hand. I looked over at him in confusion.

When he saw my expression, he was quick to say, "Don't misread any of this. I'm definitely not trying to come onto you. I can't give you a comforting hug while I'm driving, so I figured this would be the next best thing."

I gave him a small, sad smile. "Thank you."

It wasn't much longer until we parked near a pond. There weren't any houses nearby, and it was near a wooded area. There were a few trees near the edge of the pond. Bowie exited the car, and I quickly climbed out too. He was already walking towards the pond, so I jogged to catch up to him. Once I fell into step beside him, I asked, "Why did you bring me here?"

He sighed and said, "Because you're going through something devastating right now. When I'm dealing with emotions that are difficult to process, I sit out here. It's relaxing."

He sat near the edge, under a tree. I stood beside him until he grabbed my hand and pulled me down beside him. I hugged my knees into my chest, rested my chin on my knees, and watched the wind blow ripples across the surface of the water. It was serene. "Why did you start coming out here?"

Bowie picked up a rock and skipped it across the water's surface. "I didn't know how to deal with my sister dying."

I turned my head to look at him. He looked so serious. Thinking about everything that had happened that day, how supportive he'd been, I started seeing Bowie in a different light. It was strange to think he was the same boy who had thrown that note at Joshua. I scooted closer to him and rested my head on his shoulder and mumbled, "I'm sorry. I had no idea."

He leaned his head against mine and said, "It's okay. It happened a few years ago. Drunk driving accident. It still hits me sometimes, and I just come out here and sit."

"Am I ever going to feel like I can breathe again?"

"Eventually."

We sat out there until the sun set. I numbly followed him back to the car, and he drove me home. The drive was silent, and I wished it would last forever. I dreaded the moment I would step into that empty house. I didn't want to be there without them. The drive didn't last nearly as long as I had hoped. I didn't make any move to exit the car once he parked. I looked over at him. "It's going to be so quiet in there," I whispered.

"I know, and I know you don't wanna be here alone. I promise it won't be for long. I'm going to go find Osbourne and bring him here. You won't have to stay here alone."

I leaned over the console and hugged him. He hugged back as I whispered, "Thank you. You're a really good friend."

I let out a shaky breath before stepping out of the car and walking towards the empty house. Tears began slipping down my face as I thought how alone I would feel once

I stepped inside the house. In that moment, I didn't think things could get any worse. I couldn't have been more wrong.

Chapter 10

I brought my knees to my chest and wrapped my arms around my legs, hugging my knees closer. I rested my forehead atop my knees, and tears began pouring down my face. My body shook as I sobbed, whimpers escaping my lips. In that moment, I felt more broken than I ever had before. It felt as though my world was crumbling around me.

I had been sitting alone in my room, crying for over an hour. The longer I sat there, the more I broke. The pain I felt in those moments made me know that I was never going to be the same person I was when I woke up that morning. I was never going to be that same girl who had been so happy. I was broken, and at that moment, I couldn't see myself being fixed ever again.

I felt a warm hand rub across my upper back. An arm draped around my shoulder, and I knew it was him. He pulled me into his side in a silent attempt to comfort me. I took a shaky breath as I tried to calm down. I didn't want to cry in front of him. I didn't want to break like this in front of him.

He pulled my hair back, behind my shoulders and stated, "It's okay to cry. You don't have to feel ashamed to cry in front of me."

I lifted my head off my knees, and with a tear-soaked face, I looked at him. I knew I looked just as broken as I felt. "I don't want any pity."

"I'm not here to pity you," He began as he dried my face with the sleeves of his shirt. "I'm here to comfort you. I won't say anything if you don't want me to. I'm just here because you're hurting, and you shouldn't have to face pain alone."

I wrapped my arms around his neck and pulled myself closer to him, unconsciously climbing into his lap. He wrapped his arms around my waist and held me tightly. I pulled away to look into his eyes. He reached a hand up to caress my cheek, and I leaned into his hand. He leaned in closer, and I did too. I closed my eyes and pressed my lips against his. With his lips against mine, I could forget all that had happened. At least, for a little while.

I tangled my fingers into his hair and pulled him closer to me, deepening the kiss. He held me firmly against him. I ran my tongue against his lower lip as the kiss became more heated. He slipped a hand under my shirt and ran his hand against my bare back. Shivers ran up my spine, and I quietly moaned against his lips. He gently laid me on the floor and pulled away, hovering over me. He looked down at me with an intense and serious expression.

"I don't want to take advantage of your vulnerable state." He took a breath and rephrased what he was trying to say. "I don't want to do this if you're only using it as a distraction from what happened."

My heart broke a little at the realization that he feared I was using him to distract myself from the pain I was feeling.

I gently caressed his cheek, and tears brimmed my eyes. I cleared my throat.

"I don't know what to say to that."

He pulled my hand away, teary eyed, and said, "You don't have to say anything."

He stood up and walked away. The tears began to flow again as I lay there and watched him leave. My heart broke more in that moment than it ever had before. In that moment, I felt truly alone. More alone than I ever had before. In that moment, watching him leave, it felt like a "goodbye." One that I never expected to come. One that I wished would never come. I sobbed at the loss of the one person I couldn't stand to lose.

Losing my parents had hurt more than I could imagine, but in the back of my mind, I felt that I'd be okay with Osbourne in my life. He made me feel so many wonderful things. As he walked away, all of those wonderful things went with him. I lost the person I thought would hold me together through all of this. I didn't know how I was going to survive all of this, and a part of me didn't expect to survive it.

Chapter 11

ach day passed in a blur, and before I knew it, it was the day of the funeral. I was numb and barely processed all of the people who were coming and going, giving their condolences. I stood alone at the front of the room near the caskets for most of the visitation before my uncle and his kids arrived.

"Zdravo, Delta," my uncle greeted.

"Zdravo," I repeated back before adding, "I don't know much Serbian."

He shook his head in what seemed to be disappointment. "I always told Nikita he need teach you Serbian," he mumbled in a thick Serbian accent.

My uncle, Nicholai, had always been proud to be Serbian. My father always said that Nicholai regretted moving with him to America. He would always comment on how he dreamed of returning home, but he couldn't afford to move back to Serbia. He would say that he was stuck with the foolish Americans. He always looked down on my father for marrying an American woman and adopting American customs.

"You remember your cousins: Damir, Janika, and Svetlana," he motioned to them.

"My dad has pictures of all of you."

Nicholai grunted in response before turning to his kids and speaking with them in Serbian. I stood uncomfortably, feeling like an outsider.

More people came through, offering their condolences to each of us. Nicholai occasionally muttering to himself about the foolish Americans. I stood stiffly, wishing for all of this to end and trying to keep my thoughts from filling with Osbourne. I wished he'd come to comfort me, but I dreaded seeing him again after the way he left. I wished any of my friends would come. Any familiar face that might alleviate the mind-numbing pain I was feeling. As the visitation was drawing to a close and the funeral was about to begin, I felt a weight in my chest as I hadn't seen any of my friends. Just as I was about to find a seat, I spotted Bowie. He rushed in with a woman following him. He shook hands with my uncle and cousins before pulling me into a hug.

"I'm so sorry I'm so late. My mom wanted to come, so I had to wait for her to get off work."

I wrapped my arms around him and mumbled, "I'm really glad you made it."

He pulled back and looked at me with furrowed eyebrows. "I'm surprised Jack isn't up here with you."

"He probably isn't coming. It's a long story," I waved off as tears began welling up in my eyes. "I'll tell you later," I added as I wiped the tears away.

"Okay," he said, looking at me in concern.

"You must be Bowie's mom." I turned my attention to the woman behind Bowie. "I'm Delta."

She pulled me in a hug. "Marissa. It's so nice to finally meet you. I've heard a lot about you from the boys. I'm so sorry for your losses."

I cleared my throat and muttered, "Thank you."

"If you need anything, anything at all, just say the word. You are always welcome in my home."

I gave her a sad smile and said, "I might have to take you up on that offer. I really don't like staying in that house all alone."

"You've been staying there alone?" She asked in shock.

I nodded as tears began spilling down my face.

She pulled me in another hug and said, "You won't be tonight. You'll come home with us."

I took a shaky breath and said, "Thank you."

After the interaction with Bowie and his mom, everyone took their seats and the service began. I couldn't focus on anything the minister said. The only thing going through my mind was, "I'm never going to see my parents again. I'm never going to hear my dad yell that I'm going to be late for school again. He's never going to call me a krava again. I'm never going to have movie nights with them. No more family dinners. No more holidays with them. My mom is never going to make me soup when I'm sick again. No more baking cookies with her when I'm upset. All the things I thought I would experience with them, gone." I was so broken and lost, and I didn't know how to fix it.

I was pulled from these thoughts when the service ended, and we were ushered out to the parking lot. I sat alone in the family limo that was provided by the funeral home. My uncle opted to drive his family to the cemetery himself. I cried alone the entire drive there.

I felt numb as the minister spoke, prayed, and read the Bible at the burial site. It all passed in a blur, and I barely registered when Joshua and Violet walked up to me.

Joshua pulled me into a hug and whispered, "I'm so sorry, Del." He pulled away before speaking at a louder volume. "Marco tried to come, but he was too emotional. He was worried it would make you more upset. I tried to convince him to come with me and ended up coming late. I made it in time for the service. Violet rode with me."

Violet took that opportunity to voice how sorry she was. She hugged me, "I can't imagine how you're feeling. I wish I could make it better."

I cleared my throat and said, "Thanks."

Joshua asked, "Are you staying with family?"

I shook my head. "I've been staying at the house by myself, but I'm staying over at Bowie's house tonight. His mom insists."

Joshua nodded. He opened his mouth to speak but stopped, as if he were trying to find the right words to say. He sighed and spoke, "I have to ask. Where's Osbourne?"

Tears brimmed in my eyes. "Not here, and I don't want to talk about it." I wiped my eyes and glanced around until I spotted Bowie and Marissa. "Um...I'm gonna go. I'll see you guys at school."

I quickly turned and walked away before they could respond. As I approached Bowie and Marissa, Marissa wrapped her arm around my shoulders, pulling me into a side hug. She guided me in the direction of Bowie's car. "I'm so sorry, Hun. I know this isn't easy. Do you need to pick up clothes from your house?"

I shook my head. "I really don't want to go back there at all right now."

She nodded. "I understand. You can borrow some of Bowie's clothes."

"Thanks for offering her my wardrobe, Mom," Bowie muttered sarcastically from the other side of me.

She ignored his comment. "We'll order pizza and watch movies. I'll buy a bunch of junk, and we can all just eat our feelings tonight."

I sniffled and muttered, "That sounds nice."

Chapter 12

Marissa dropped Bowie and me off at their house. Bowie lent me some sweatpants and a t-shirt, and after I changed, he led me to the living room and showed me his DVD collection. We were silently picking out movies to watch. I kept stealing glances at him every so often. It was strange to me that we had been spending so much time together, but it felt natural. I was grateful to have him since Osbourne wasn't going to be around anymore.

Bowie cleared his throat and asked, "So, are we going to talk about whatever happened with you and Jack?"

My chest felt tight, and I struggled to push down the heartache I felt. "I don't really want to, but I think we have to. Don't we?"

He turned to me and grabbed my arm, pulling my attention to him. I looked at him, and he looked worried. I looked into his eyes, and tears welled up in mine. A strangled sob left my chest as the tears fell from my eyes. He pulled me into his chest, holding me tightly as I sobbed on his shoulder. He rubbed my back in an attempt to comfort me. It only made me sob harder. All of the emotions I had been trying so hard to suppress were released.

"Hey," he whispered in my ear, "it's okay. Everything is gonna be okay."

I took a deep breath and pulled away. He held my shoulders, and I looked at him, tears still flowing down my face. "How do you know that? My parents are gone. Ozzie is gone. Who the hell is gonna make cookies with me now?"

Bowie pulled me into him as I began sobbing again. "It's going to be okay because you're not alone. You have other people who care about you. And as for making cookies, fuck, Del. I'll make cookies with you."

I nodded against his shoulder, slowly calming down. "I don't wanna make cookies right now. I miss Mom too much."

He chuckled, "Well, we don't have to make them right now. I'll make cookies with you anytime you want. And I mean that. If you get upset at two in the morning and want to make cookies, I'm just a phone call away. Hell, you can just show up here and drag my ass out of bed."

I pulled away, chuckling. I wiped my face on the sleeves of my sweater. Taking a deep, shaky breath, I smiled sadly at him. "Thanks."

He ruffled my hair and said, "Anytime."

I sighed sadly. "Things are over between me and Ozzy."

"What happened?"

"I don't know. Assumptions, misunderstandings. Small things happening at the wrong time, meaning he's not here when it matters the most."

"I need a little clarification here."

I told Bowie everything that had happened the last time I saw Osbourne, my face turning bright red when I alluded to the intimate moment that ultimately ended things. Saying it all aloud made it feel so final, and my heart broke again. In that moment, I felt so empty. Too much had happened in such a short period of time, and I knew I'd never be the same.

After a moment, Bowie asked, "You don't think explaining things will fix anything?"

Tears fell from my eyes as I looked at him. "If he had shown up today, I would think so. But I needed him today, and he wasn't there. I can't let that go."

He nodded and said, "I understand. He should've been there today."

"What makes it hurt so much more, I knew he wouldn't come, but I still hoped that he would."

He looked at me with sad eyes. "Delta, maybe it's a good thing he didn't come."

"What do you mean?" I asked, shakily.

He sighed, looked away, and ran his hand through his hair. "You guys were just getting started with your relationship. Relying on someone to fix the amount of grief you're experiencing isn't a healthy way to begin a relationship. I get that he makes you feel good, and he makes you happy. I know you just wanted him to be there for you, but I think you might benefit more to navigate this without him."

"You think I should face losing my parents on my own?" I asked as an overwhelming feeling of loneliness filled my chest.

"That's not really what I meant." He sighed heavily. "I'm not the greatest at explaining things. I just mean that you're going to have to relearn how to live. Your daily routine is never going to be the same, and it might be easier to learn how to live again if you don't have someone to fill your mind with and push away the grief. You have to face it at some point, and it's better to face it sooner rather than later. Does that make sense?"

I nodded, looking down at my feet. "Yeah, I get what you're saying."

"I wish you didn't have to go through all of this. It really sucks."

I surprised him by wrapping my arms around him and hugging him tightly. "I'm really glad I at least have you to tell me all of this. It helps a lot."

He hugged me back and mumbled, "Anytime."

We pulled away, and we just looked at each other. He pushed some hair out of my face and tucked it behind my ear. Suddenly, we heard the front door open and close. We quickly pulled away from each other and walked into the kitchen to see Marissa setting grocery bags down on the table. She had really gone crazy buying a bunch of junk food.

"Here are some snacks for tonight, and I'll order some pizza. Did you two pick out some movies to watch tonight?"

"Yeah, we picked out a few," Bowie answered.

"Sweet. What kind of pizza do you kids want?"

"Pepperoni," Bowie and I said at the same time.

"Pepperoni, easy enough. Why don't you two get the snacks and movie set up while I go get my laptop and order the pizza?"

"Okay," I mumbled while Bowie said, "Sure."

We carried all the Walmart bags into the living room and dumped the snacks onto the coffee table. There were Doritos, plain Lays, barbeque Lays, a giant bag of MnM's, Twizzlers, pretzels, Veggie Straws, and a variety bag of Hershey's chocolates. "Does your mom normally buy stuff like this for movie nights?"

"No. She was probably trying to make sure she had something you like. She should've just asked what kind of snacks you like."

"So, what does she normally buy?"

"Chips and Twizzlers."

I couldn't help but laugh at how much extra junk she had bought. "She really went overboard then."

Bowie chuckled and said, "Definitely."

"Okay, pizza is ordered." Marissa stood in the doorway, looking at us with concern. "Please tell me you like at least one of those snacks."

I smiled at her and said, "I like most of these snacks."

She sighed before walking over and plopping down beside me on the couch. "Thank goodness. I was worried I screwed up because I forgot to ask you what you liked."

"You know, if you wanted to know what she liked, you could've called," Bowie teased his mom.

"I didn't think of that, Smarty-pants."

I chuckled at their bickering, and for a moment, I didn't feel so broken and alone.

We spent the night watching movie after movie. Marissa went to bed around 11:00, but Bowie and I stayed up much later. For the first time since my parents died, I didn't have

trouble falling asleep. I didn't spend hours lying awake, crying, and thinking about all the things my parents would miss
out on. It was the first night I didn't have to feel like my entire
life was falling apart.

Chapter 13

The day that I moved in with my foster family, I felt so numb. The days had all blurred together, and I felt empty and numb. While I assumed the Smiths were a wonderful family, I had no desire to try to become a part of that family.

Evangeline and Earnest Smith weren't one of those couples who had trouble conceiving and were desperate for a child. They already had two kids of their own: a boy and a girl. They were just a couple who wanted to do their part to make the world a little better. Upon meeting them, they seemed like a happy, normal family, but to a girl who had just lost her family, their happy family was suffocating.

Moving into their home was stiff and uncomfortable. I didn't want to be in their home. Earnest and Evangeline often tried to spark conversation with me, but they were always deterred with brief answers in a clipped tone. Destiny often asked if I would play with her, but I always said, "Maybe later." Sometimes I would feel a pang of guilt when I would watch the glimmer of hope fade from the eight-year-old's eyes. Phoenix, the thirteen-year-old, would always swoop the girl up in his arms with the promise to play with her while glaring at me with judgmental eyes.

Being in their home, I felt out of place. It was like I was a puzzle piece that fell into the wrong puzzle box. I looked like I should belong, but I just didn't fit. The closer you looked at me, compared to the other pieces, the more obvious it became that I didn't belong. My presence was just wrong. As much as the Smiths tried to make me fit into their life, I just didn't, and I didn't want to pretend that I did. I often exiled myself to my bedroom to avoid the uncomfortable feel of being forced into their lives.

When sitting alone in my room, my mind alternated between thoughts of my parents and thoughts of Osbourne. I couldn't help but focus on Osbourne and push away the—now painful—memories of my parents. I suppose I thought if I didn't think about them, life without them would hurt less.

That night, my thoughts turned to Osbourne. I missed the way he held me. I missed the way the corners of his lips twitched so slightly when he teased me and was trying not to smile. I missed waking up to the smell of his cologne whenever we fell asleep while studying. I missed his presence. Without him, I felt so empty and cold. So alone. I never knew I could feel so broken. Before losing my parents, before Osbourne, I never understood how a person could be alive but feel dead inside. Being swallowed up by your own emotions and trapped in your own hopeless thoughts is the loneliest, most suffocating place to be, and the further you burrow into it, the harder it is to climb back out.

Chapter 14

After spending the past months with Ozzy, it felt strange, lonely, without him by my side now. Even walking down the hallway at school felt lonely. I still had my friends, but it wasn't the same. Being with them, after everything that had happened, almost felt forced. The loss of my parents had left me feeling empty, but with Osbourne gone too, I felt like a puppet being pulled along through each day, feeling nothing but strings tugging me forward.

Glancing down the hallway, I saw Osbourne standing at the lockers with Bowie and Arvin. Nothing about them seemed out of place. Why was it so easy for him to return to his life before us, but I struggled to even socialize with the friends that I'd had my whole life? It wasn't fair. None of this was.

I turned away when Bowie caught me watching them. I quickly gathered the books I needed from my locker, slammed the locker door shut, and turned down the hall, all but sprinting to my next class. I silently wished that Osbourne would follow me, stop me from walking away. Each step further I took, my heart broke a little more. I took a deep, shuddering breath, pushing my emotions down, before stepping into the classroom.

The day was passing in a blur, and before I knew it, it was time for lunch. I sat in silence while my friends delved into conversations with each other. Every now and then, I noticed Joshua looking over at me. I knew he was worried about me, but there were no words to make him understand how I was feeling inside. A tug on my sleeve pulled me out of my thoughts. I looked down at my sleeve, then up at Violet.

"What's up?" I asked.

"I feel like we haven't hung out in forever."

I bit my lip anxiously and nodded. "Things have been pretty hectic lately."

Violet looked at me sadly. "I meant before...you know."

I nodded, appreciating that she didn't mention my parents. I sighed before pulling my phone out. I sent Violet a text, asking her if I could come over to her house after school before following up with a text clarifying that I wanted just the two of us to hang out. She smiled down at her phone before sending a thumbs-up emoji. Nervousness filled my chest at the thought of going over to her house. Something I'd done a million times before, but somehow, it felt different now. Things were different now. I couldn't help thinking how strange it was to feel nervous over hanging out with someone who had once been one of my closest friends.

The bell rang, pulling me away from my thoughts on my nervousness. I mumbled, "See you later," to Violet before scurrying off to my locker. As I approached my locker and put more distance between me and my friends, relief washed over me. The feeling surprised me for a moment before the realization dawned on me. It wasn't every person at that table that made me feel nervous and out of place. It was one person. Scarlet. I was afraid of what she might say about Osbourne or my parents.

I began pulling everything I would need for English out of my locker when I felt someone nudge my elbow. I turned my head to the side to glance at Joshua as I continued grabbing the things I needed. Sympathy covered his features as he spoke, "You doing okay?"

I shrugged and mumbled, "As good as I can."

"That doesn't sound very reassuring."

"It's not meant to be reassuring. I'm just trying to be honest with you about how I'm doing."

"Fair enough," he mumbled back as we made our way towards the English classroom.

Joshua and I sat in our usual seats, and it wasn't long before our teacher began the lecture. I scribbled in my notebook, not really listening to anything being said. It had been the same in my other classes. I just couldn't focus, and I wished I were anywhere else. As the class dragged on, a balled up piece of paper landed on my desk, pulling me from my scribbling. I looked at the ball inquisitively before lifting my gaze to scan the room for who may have thrown the paper ball. My gaze fell on Bowie, who motioned for me to open the ball.

With furrowed brows, I straightened out the paper and read the message scrawled across:

"Talk after class?"

I glanced back up at Bowie, who was watching me closely. I looked back at the paper and sighed. I looked back at him and gave him a thumbs-up in agreement to talking after class.

I began tapping my pencil against my notebook as I began wondering what he might want to talk about. An uneasiness settled in the pit of my stomach as I wondered if Osbourne would be with him. I glanced in his direction, and my heart clenched at the sight of him. Once tears began pooling in my eyes, I forced my attention away from him. I clenched my shaky hands and took a shaky breath. As I exhaled, I mentally told myself that it would be fine.

Class ended too soon for my liking, and Joshua and I gathered up our things and walked out of the room. Joshua gave me a side hug and promised to check-in on me later and continued on as I stood in front of my locker. As I focused on gathering what I needed for my next class, someone leaned against the locker beside me. Without looking away from what I was doing, I said, "Hi, Bowie."

"Del."

I pulled out my notebook and closed my locker door, turning my attention to Bowie, who smirked at me.

"What?"

He shook his head and pushed off the locker he'd been leaning on. "Nothing," he said as he wrapped his arm around my shoulders and began guiding me in the direction of my next class. "Can't I walk a friend to class without my motives being questioned?"

"Nope, absolutely not. Very out of character for you," I stated flatly.

"Okay, fine. I just wanted to check on you, see how you're holding up." He pulled me to a stop just outside of the classroom I needed to go in. He crossed his arms and leaned back against the wall, watching me as he waited for an answer.

I sighed and looked away from him. "I've been placed in a foster home, and the only house I've ever lived in is being sold."

"I'm sure that's all difficult to process."

I looked at him as my chest felt tight and nodded. "Can we not talk about stuff like this at school?" I asked as I looked away, tears forming in my eyes.

"Yeah, sorry. I just hadn't heard from you, and I wanted to check in."

I cleared my throat as I tried to swallow down the emotions that threatened to drown me. "Well, you could always text or call me. That's a good way to check-in without bringing me to tears in the hallway at school."

He chuckled and nodded, "Yeah, I'll try that next time. I guess I didn't think you'd be honest with me unless I asked face-to-face."

I smiled sadly and replied, "Yeah, you're probably right."

"I should probably get to class," he muttered as he began walking away. Before I walked into the classroom, he stopped and called back to me, "Del, don't push yourself too hard. It's okay to not be okay."

I stared at him for a moment before nodding and walking into the classroom.

Chapter 15

Walking into Violet's house seemed so foreign now. We walked in and through the house in silence. As we entered her room, she broke the silence. "Things are weird. I know it's not just me. Things are weird with you and everyone now, and they have been since you and Osbourne."

"I don't mean for them to be," I mumbled under my breath.

"I'm not blaming you, Dee. I'm just saying that things are weird, and I wish they weren't. I know you had big plans to leave us all behind after graduation, but I miss my best friend."

I looked over at her. She was sitting on her bed with her knees pulled up to her chest, and I had never seen her look so sad before. Guilt swelled in my chest. I had pushed her and Marco away because Scarlet didn't like Osbourne. It wasn't intentional. I just knew they weren't willing to stand up to Scarlet, and I didn't want to listen to Scarlet's opinions on Osbourne.

I sat next to her on the bed and wrapped my arm around her shoulders. Quietly I said, "I'm sorry, Vi. I didn't mean to bail on you. I just didn't want to deal with Scarlet making me feel bad about something that made me happy."

She nodded and squeaked, "I get it." We were silent for a moment before she spoke again. "What happened between you and Osbourne?"

I let out a shaky breath as the tears formed. "We had a sort-of fight that was caused by a misunderstanding."

"Misunderstandings are fixable," she voiced, hopeful.

I nodded as the tears fell. "They are," I began as emotion filled my voice, "But missing out on the funeral for my parents and not checking on me isn't."

"He hasn't checked on you at all?"

I began sobbing as I shook my head. "You have, Joshua, Marco, and even Bowie, but he hasn't."

Violet wrapped her arms around me and pulled me into a hug and rubbed my back. "I'm sorry, Dee. I don't know what else to say, but I'm sorry."

Half an hour. That's how long I sobbed while Violet comforted me. All the nervousness and awkwardness between us was gone, and it was like nothing had changed between us. It was like we hadn't spent any time apart. It was comfortable. I still felt dead and empty, but at least I took back an important friendship.

Chapter 16

After leaving Violet's, I didn't want to go back to my foster home, so I started walking. I didn't know where I was going. I just started walking aimlessly. I didn't stop until I came to a cliff, looking out over the sea. While sitting with Violet should have left me feeling comforted, or at the very least, not so alone, I didn't. Standing there, the loneliness washed over me again, and I felt empty and alone again.

stood at the edge of the cliff, wind whipping my hair in every direction. I closed my eyes and breathed in deeply. I let out a shaky breath, and tears threatened to fall. My chest tightened, and I was, once again, feeling overwhelmed by emotion. I wanted to let go. I wanted to fall forward and to the ocean below. I wanted to drown my worries and sorrows. I wanted to bury all the pain that had begun to follow me everywhere I went.

I took a step closer to the edge, and tears began to pour. I knew I had no one left to save me. No one left for me to pretend for. No one to pull me back. A whimper erupted from my chest as I stepped even closer, now feeling the broken edges of rock and dirt at the cliff's edge. One more step, and it would all end. I took a deep, shaky breath and prepared to take the last step. I began to step forward as I shed a few final tears. Before I could free fall to the ocean below, I felt a pair of arms wrap around my waist and pull me back. Whoever had grabbed me lost balance, and we both fell back with me landing on their chest.

I was hastily pushed off the person and pinned to the ground. He hovered over me, fury covering every inch of his face. He yelled, "What the hell were you thinking?!"

Tears streamed down my face, and I felt empty. I emotionlessly asked, "Do you care?"

Hurt replaced the anger, and he stood up. He began walking away from me for the second time. Processing what had just happened, I hopped up and angrily stomped over to him. I grabbed his wrist and pulled him to a stop.

"Who are you to stop me, then get mad and leave again? You walked away first. You don't get to be mad at me for my choices. Not when all you're going to do is keep walking away from me like everyone else in my life."

He ran his hand through his hair and chuckled bitterly. "You really think I walked away from you before? It was pretty clear to me that you were just using me as a distraction from all the bullshit in your life."

I felt my heart break all over again from hearing that statement. I turned my back to him so that he wouldn't see my tears and took a shaky breath. "I never said that."

"You didn't have to."

"You're really a dumbass sometimes," I mumbled.

He grabbed my arm and turned me back to face him and snapped, "Excuse me? I'm the dumbass."

His anger eased as he took in the tears streaming down my face. "Yeah, you're the dumbass. You're a dumbass for thinking my silence meant you were right. You're a dumbass for thinking that I would use you. You're a dumbass for not realizing that I was quiet because it broke my heart knowing that you thought that I would use you like that. You're a dumbass for not realizing how much you broke my heart when you walked away. But you know what? I'm the bigger dumbass for actually letting myself get close to you and actually letting myself fall in love with you. I'm the dumbass for thinking that you actually would surprise me and be there for me when my parents died. I'm the biggest dumbass for actually believing that you loved me too."

I pulled away from him, and this time, I was the one who walked away. I began my walk home, and not once did I look back.

Chapter 17

It had been three days since that day with Osbourne on the cliff. I hadn't been back to school. I told Evangeline that I needed a little more time away from school. After discussing with Earnest, they decided to let me stay home the rest of the week, but I had to start back the following Monday.

Once Phoenix and Destiny left for school and Earnest and Evangeline for work, I would sneak out and just walk around. I never had a plan on what I would do or where I would go. I would just start walking. It wasn't until the third day that I ended up somewhere I shouldn't have been. It was a little past where Osbourne lived, in a terrible neighborhood. That was the day I met Zen and his friends.

They were sitting around a picnic table near the skatepark. I wasn't going to stop. I was just going to walk past them. But someone yelled a vulgar comment about my "nice ass" at me, and I stopped in my tracks and turned around. I stomped over to them and snapped, "Who the hell said that?"

The smell of marijuana wafted from them as I glared at the small group of people. One of the boys chuckled and pointed at the other boy sat there and said, "It was him."

I turned my harsh gaze onto the culprit, and his eyes widened. He looked at the boy who spoke and snipped, "Why'd you rat me out, Zen?"

He chuckled again and said, "Because she looks pissed, and I'm not getting my ass beat over you."

"What's your name?" I snapped at the boy.

He turned his attention back to me and hesitated. "Havoc," he mumbled.

"Well, Havoc, what was it you wanted to do to me and my ass?"

Zen began laughing loudly as the color drained from Havoc's face.

When Havoc didn't respond, I spoke again. "What's wrong? You can only make vulgar comments when the girl is walking away, but you don't have the balls to say anything to her face?"

My statement elicited more laugher from Zen and caused Havoc's face to flush bright red.

Once his laugher calmed, Zen spoke. "I like you. What's your name?"

I looked at him for a moment, debating whether to continue this interaction or to walk away. Finally, I answered, "Delta."

"Delta, I'm Zen. You've met Havoc," he began motioning and introducing me to the people around the table, "That's Tess and Jewel."

"You smoke?" Jewel asked.

I shook my head as I looked at the joint in her hand.

Tess and Jewel looked at each other before Tess spoke. "Do you want to?"

If I had been asked that question a month ago, I wouldn't have even considered it. Before losing my parents, I would've said no in a heartbeat. But they weren't here to be disappointed. They weren't here to tell me that I shouldn't be doing things like that or socializing with people who do.

After a moment of consideration, I stepped towards Jewel and said, "Sure."

That was another turning point in my life. That was the first choice that would send me further into a downward spiral as my life continued to fall apart.

Chapter 18

I t was now Sunday, and I only had the day left until I would have to return to school and face everyone again. I had been meeting up with Zen, Havoc, Tess, and Jewel everyday since I met them. We all smoked together at the skatepark then walked around the neighborhood.

"Starting tomorrow, I won't be able to hangout with you guys until after school lets out," I announced to the group.

"Laaame!" Tess shouted.

I chuckled at her. "Sorry, but I have to go."

"Why?" Havoc asked.

"Uhh..." I hesitated. "That's a good question. Because I'm supposed to, I guess," I chuckled out.

"Let me guess, parents have high expectations," Havoc said with a raised eyebrow.

At the mention of my parents, I stopped in my tracks, and it felt as though I'd been punched in the chest. Zen looked over me with concern on his face. I shook my head, "No, no parents. I'm not really sure what my foster parents expect of me either."

"Shit," Havoc stated, looking panicked. "I didn't know you were an orphan."

I looked at him with furrowed eyebrows. "That's the first time someone has come out and called me an orphan."

Zen cleared his throat and asked, "Was it recent?"

I nodded, "Yeah. It was pretty recent."

"Like this year?" Havoc asked.

"This year, last month," I mumbled back.

"Ah man, I feel like shit." Havoc rubbed the back of his neck.

"Don't worry about it. You didn't know," I assured.

"So, you go back to school tomorrow," Zen interrupted.

"Yeah. Definitely not looking forward to it."

"Are there at least hot guys to look at?" Jewel asked.

I chuckled dryly. "Well, my recent ex is there."

"How recent?" Tess inquired.

"Right after the parents died," I stated.

"Damn. You're having a really shitty time lately," Havoc said.

"Yeah, things have been pretty shitty lately," I chuckled.

"Things end badly?" Zen asked.

"It definitely wasn't good."

"Did he at least have the decency to go to the funeral and check on you?" Jewel asked.

"Nope," I said before adding, "But his best friend did."

"Is he hot?" Tess asked with a mischievous grin.

I laughed and said, "He's not bad looking."

"Good enough to be eye candy throughout the school day?" Jewel asked suggestively.

"I don't know about that. He's been a good friend to me through everything."

"Boyfriends that started out as just friends are always the best," Jewel stated.

"I agree, but there's not going to be another boyfriend for a long time," I replied.

"Enough about boyfriends. What you need is a 'special' buddy," Havoc suggested with hand quotes.

"I have a feeling I'm going to regret asking this. What's a 'special' buddy?" I responded.

"A friend with fun benefits," he said while wiggling his eyebrows.

I laughed and smacked his shoulder. "You're disgusting. I'm not looking for a friend with benefits, you pervert."

"Hey, I didn't mean me. I think you and Zen would be much better suited for fooling around. You guys would click better."

"You think Zen and I should be friends with benefits?" I asked in amusement with a raised eyebrow.

"As hot as Delta is, I don't think that's a good idea," Zen commented.

"And why is that?" Tess asked with a mischievous smirk.

"Because sleeping with a friend is always a bad idea. If someone catches feelings, it ruins the friendship."

"So you're saying if Delta came onto you, you wouldn't sleep with her?" Tess asked, smugly.

"No, I'd definitely sleep with her if she came onto me."

"Okay, I don't know whether to be flattered or disturbed," I interrupted. "Can we redirect the conversation away from my sex life?"

"Fine, Prude," Tess rolled her eyes at me.

"If you decide to cut class and wanna hangout, you know where to find us." Jewel invited.

"Yeah, yeah," I dismissed with the wave of my hand. "I should start heading home."

"I'll walk with you," Zen offered as he stood up.

Collective "ooo's" could be heard from the table as we walked away. I lifted up my middle finger to them, and Zen chuckled under his breath.

"You really didn't have to walk with me, you know."

"I know I didn't. I wanted to."

I glanced at him. He had his hood flipped up, and his hands were tucked into his hoodie pockets. A chuckle left my lips as I teased, "Trying to work your way into being my 'special' buddy?"

He laughed and shook his head. "No, but that's not a bad idea."

"Is that your smooth way of letting me know that you want in my pants?"

"That's my smooth way of saying I'm not trying to get into your pants, but I'm not opposed to the idea of being in your pants."

I looked closely at him for a moment, soaking in his features. His skin was fair but not too pale. His hair was a darker brown color, and it looked nice with his hazel eyes.

"Okay, have I made things weird? Because I don't want things to be weird between us." He stopped walking and had a nervous expression across his face.

I smiled and shook my head, "No, zero weirdness. I guess I was just wondering if I would ever come onto you."

He smiled back at me, "And?"

"Too early to say," I smirked mischievously and started walking again.

He laughed as he followed behind me. It wasn't much longer before we stood outside of my foster parents' house. "Well, this is me."

He stared at the two-story house. "That's a nice house."

"Yeah, my foster parents have good jobs, I guess. I don't really know much about them. I mostly stay in my room when I'm here."

He eyed me inquisitively.

I started rambling. "I mean, they seem like very nice people, but they already have two kids of their own. They have a happy family, and I feel out of place here. I had my own happy family, and they just remind me of what I lost."

"Hey, you don't have to explain to me. I'm here if you wanna talk, but don't feel like you have to explain yourself."

I smiled at him and pulled him into a hug. "Thanks, Zen."

He hugged me back and mumbled, "No problem."

I pulled away and turned to go into the house, but he stopped me. "Let me see your phone."

"Uhh, okay." I unlocked my phone and handed it to him. After a moment, he handed it back to me. "What did you do?"

"I added my number in. In case you need anything."

I smiled at him as he walked away.

I walked inside and up to my room. I pulled out an already-rolled-joint that Tess had given me and the lighter Jewel gave me. I opened my window and lit the joint. I was quickly becoming addicted to my new habit. I laid on my bed, staring at the ceiling, letting my mind drift out of focus.

The fog that filled my head pushed away the pain I had been feeling, and numbness crept over me. I felt as though I were sinking into my mattress, and in that moment, I didn't think I would ever move from that spot. My habit was quickly replacing the friends I no longer felt close to. It became the comfort I thought I would have from Osbourne. A tingly feeling spread throughout my body, and I let my eyelids fall closed. It didn't take long for me to drift off to sleep.

Chapter 19

W alking into school that morning was enough for me. I took one look at Osbourne, and he took one step in my direction. That's all it took for me to turn around and walk out the doors. I ran through the parking lot and away from the school. I fell into a brisk walk as I headed down the sidewalk, my breathing heavy as I tried to catch my breath. I pulled out my phone and called Zen.

"Hey, aren't you supposed to be in school?" he asked in amusement.

"I couldn't do it. I took one look at him, and he took one step in my direction. I couldn't do it. Not today. Maybe I'll try again tomorrow, but not today," I blurted out hysterically.

"Woah," he said in surprise. "Just calm down. Where are you? I'll pick you up."

"Um..." I stopped and looked around. "I'm not too far from my house. I'll meet you there."

"Okay, I'll see you soon."

It wasn't long before I was approaching my house, and I saw Zen sitting in his car in the driveway. I quickly climbed into the passenger seat. I glanced at him and breathed out, "Hey."

He smirked at me. "Hey. So much for going to school, huh?"

I rolled my eyes. "Just drive."

He chuckled and backed out of the driveway.

We met up with Havoc and Jewel at a different park than we usually did. I recognized the area, and I realized it wasn't too far from Bowie's house. I didn't think much of it.

"Yay! I'm so happy you came, Del," Jewel threw her arms around me, pulling me into a tight embrace.

I chuckled and slipped my arm around her waist, returning her hug. "Yeah, it was too soon to go back to school."

"Their loss is our gain," she smiled at me.

"What are we doing today?" I asked, glancing at each person.

Havoc shrugged and suggested, "Get high and push each other on the swings."

Jewel busted out in a fit of giggles. "That sounds fun."

I raised an eyebrow at her before making eye contact with Zen and said, "Seems like someone has already checked off getting high."

"Jewel is always high," Zen chuckled.

"That's because I get high on life," Jewel announced as she spun herself in a circle. We all laughed at her comment.

That's how we spent our day. Smoking and pushing each other on the swings, and of course, Havoc left at one point to buy everyone snacks. Smoking to forget my worries was quickly becoming a necessity for me at that point, and I liked forgetting everything with my new friends. They didn't look at me like they were waiting for me to fall apart. They just let me be myself.

Eventually, we decided we all should probably head our separate ways, and of course, we decided one more round of puff-puff-pass was needed. Just as I was taking my turn, someone walking by caught my eye, causing me to choke on the exhale, which did nothing but draw his attention to me.

Zen began rubbing my back while laughing. "Dude, are you okay?"

I just nodded and choked out a muffled sentence that I hoped sounded something along the lines of "I have to go."

Bowie just stared at me with a stern expression as I approached him. I was still trying to ease my coughing. Finally, he glanced behind me at my new friends before returning his attention back to me. He sighed and asked, "Do you wanna come over for a little while?"

I simply nodded and kept my head down as we turned in the direction of his house.

Bowie and I walked in silence for a while, and I wondered what he thought of who I was becoming. I never thought that I would care what he thought of me, but I did. I stopped walking and grabbed his arm, pulling him to a stop beside me. "I wish you hadn't seen me out like this." I looked at the ground.

Bowie sighed and huffed, "What are you doing with people like that, Del?"

My hands shook as I tried to keep my emotions under control, but I couldn't stop the tears. I quickly wiped them away and looked back up at him. In a shaky voice, I pleaded, "Please don't tell him. Don't tell him how I'm doing or who I'm hanging out with."

He looked at me with a sad expression. "Delta, pushing him away isn't the answer."

The tears started rolling down my cheeks. "Bowie, things are so broken...messy. We can't go back. We're beyond fixing things between us, and it's killing me. He's pushed me away just as much, and I need to let go."

"You're really okay with letting him go?"

"If I don't, I'll never be okay." With that statement, my heart broke more than I ever thought it could. More tears spilled, and my voice shook as I said, "I have too much going on. I can't juggle a relationship when I'm barely holding myself together. Right now, I'm struggling just to survive all of this."

Tears began forming in his eyes, and Bowie pulled me into a warm embrace. I sobbed into his shoulder. It felt good to finally let everything pour out of me and to have someone to hold me together. Bowie was the friend I never saw coming.

Chapter 20

B owie and I arrived at his house, and it made me remember the last time I had been there. I let out a heavy sigh and sniffled. My eyes were puffy from crying.

"Del, you'll be okay."

I turned and looked at Bowie. I gave him a sad smile and asked, "When?"

He looked thoughtful as he stood there with his hands in his pockets. "I don't know. It'll take time." I simply nodded in response.

"Del, can I ask you something?"

I looked at him inquisitively. "Is this something we should sit down for?"

"Sure," he replied before leading me to the living room.

We sat beside each other, each with one leg folded under the other and turned so that we were facing each other. We sat in silence as he seemed to be caught in thought. Finally, I cleared my throat and asked, "So what did you want to ask me?"

"Why are you hanging out with Zen and his friends?"

I furrowed my eyebrows. "How do you know Zen?"

"How do you?" he evaded.

"I asked you first," I clipped back.

"Del," he exclaimed in an exacerbated tone.

"Bowie," I snipped back. I huffed and started again, "I'll answer whatever you want if you tell me how you know Zen."

Bowie rolled his eyes and ran his hand through his hair. "Everyone around here knows Zen and his stoner pals. They're always hanging around the parks and getting high. Occasionally, they enjoy partaking in vandalism."

"What kinds of vandalism?" I asked nervously.

"Just small stuff like graffiti or taking shopping carts and leaving them in yards or crashing them into the sides of cars like they did to my mom's car."

"I'm sorry they did that," I apologized quietly.

"It's not your fault, and you weren't with them. Now, back to my original question. Why are you hanging out with them?"

I shrugged my shoulders before sighing. "I like that they don't look at me like I should fall apart, like I am falling apart. Being with them, I can forget everything for a while. They don't ask me if I'm okay every time they see me. They just let me be. We smoke; we goof off; we swing."

"You swing?"

I chuckled and smiled at him. "Yeah, that's what we did all day today. We smoked and took turns pushing each other on the swings."

"You know, when I said you shouldn't rely on someone to fix everything for you, I didn't mean replace the people in your life with pot," he teased.

I rolled my eyes. "I know. I know this isn't a good solution, and I know it very well might make things worse. But right now, it's giving me the release I need to breathe."

"How ironic that you need to smoke so that you can breathe."

I laughed before settling into silence. After a moment, I asked, "Are you mad at me?"

He furrowed his eyebrows as his gaze scanned over me. "Why would I be mad at you?"

"For hanging out with Zen and them and smoking?"

He sighed and looked away for a moment before looking me in the eyes. A serious expression washed over his features. "I don't agree with how you're handling things, but I also told you that you needed to work through this in your own way and learn to live on your own. If this is how you're working through things, then I'll respect that. The great thing about friends is you don't always have to agree and see eye-to-eye on things. I'm not mad at you. Even if I don't agree with you or particularly like your new choice of friends."

Tears welled up in my eyes and slid down my cheeks. I leaned over and pulled him in a hug. "Thank you. I was so scared you were going to be mad at me."

He pulled me closer to him and rubbed my back. He said, quietly, to me, "You don't have to worry. I'm not going anywhere. You don't have to worry about losing me too."

Chapter 21

Bowie gave me a ride home after we talked. Walking into the house, I was met with Earnest waiting for me in the kitchen. He had a look of disappointment etched across his face. I watched him carefully as I walked further into the house.

"How was school?" he asked.

"Great," I mumbled and tried to go around him and up the stairs.

"Must have been really great since you didn't go."

I stopped and turned towards him. "If you knew I didn't go, then why'd you ask?" I snipped at him.

"To see if you'd lie to me," he answered as he stood and turned to face me.

I nodded, "Why? Who cares if I'm honest or dishonest? I won't be here long since I'm almost eighteen."

"Is that really how you feel?" he asked, sounding almost hurt at my comment.

"Yeah, that's how I feel. I'm not your kid. I'm just some kid who got dumped here after her parents died. It was unexpected, and I had nowhere else to go." I blurted out, anger seeping into my voice.

"Sit down," Earnest snapped as he pointed at a stool at the island. I complied and sat down. He sat in the stool next to me. "You're not here because you have nowhere else to go. I've been waiting for you to discuss your options. Since you're almost eighteen, your opinion will be taken into consideration when deciding your placement."

"What does that mean?" I asked as uncertainty and worry washed over me.

"It means, even though Evangeline and I would love to have you in our family, you do have the option to go live with your uncle."

I looked at him in shock. "Nicholai would consider taking me?"

"He's already been contacted, and if you want to, living with him is an option." He paused before adding, "But like I said, Evangeline and I would love to have you in our family."

"Living with Nicholai would mean moving to California?"

"Yes."

"Can I have some time to think about it?"

"Of course. Take all the time you need, and until you make a decision, we're happy to have you here."

"Okay," I mumbled.

"We do need to talk about you skipping school, though. You have to go to school."

I nodded. I looked up at him and sighed. "I didn't mean to skip. I really did try to go, but I took one step in the building and saw..." I trailed off before continuing, "I just couldn't do it."

"What did you see that made you leave?"

I sighed. "You're going to think it's stupid. That I'm being stupid."

"You don't know that."

I looked at him and debated for a moment before deciding to open up to him a little. "A guy."

"This is over a boy?" He seemed puzzled by the new information.

I nodded before taking a shaky breath. "He and I were really close and things were really good between us." Tears brimmed my eyes as I took another shaky breath. "Then my parents died, and some stuff happened. It was just a stupid misunderstanding, but he wasn't there. He didn't come, and I needed him there."

"Slow down. Where didn't he come?"

The tears began pouring down my face. "The funeral. He should've been there, but he wasn't. I shouldn't have had to lose him too."

Earnest pulled me into a hug and rubbed my back while shushing me, trying to soothe me. "I'm sorry. You shouldn't have to deal with a breakup at the same time as losing your parents."

"I miss them so much," I sobbed into him.

"I know." He rubbed my back and held me tightly.

I didn't have many close moments with my foster family, but that was an important one that made me feel less like an outsider to their family.

Chapter 22

I suppose that time in my life was the time for poor decisions. I don't remember what exactly my thought process was that morning, but for whatever reason, I thought it was a good idea to take a joint to school with me. I knew it was a bad idea to leave it in my locker, so I just kept it and my lighter in my jacket pocket. The first half of the day, I just kept thinking about the joint in my pocket and how badly I wanted to smoke it. I knew it would be a bad idea to smoke the whole thing by myself at school, but I didn't know anyone at school who would smoke with me.

Lunch rolled around, and I slipped out the back doors of the school and headed for the bleachers. I sat underneath them with my legs tucked in a crisscross position. I pulled out the joint and lighter. Flicking the lighter on, I brought it up to the joint that was held tightly between my lips. As the flame engulfed the tip, I breathed deeply. There was a tickle in my throat as the smoke filled my lungs. I held the cough down as best as I could as I exhaled. Once all the smoke was out, the coughing fit began. I waved the smoke away, and just as I was about to take another hit, I heard voices drawing near. As they came closer, I realized I knew the voices.

"Dee, is it cozy under there?" Violet smirked at me.

I rolled my eyes at her and giggled. "It's actually not that bad. Bring a pillow and a blanket, and it'll be cozy enough to sleep under here." I paused then asked, "So, what are the two of you doing together?"

Violet glanced behind her at Bowie. "We were looking for you."

"Why?"

"You weren't in the cafeteria or at your locker. I was concerned. I found him in front of your locker."

I looked over at Bowie. "Why were you at my locker?"

"I wanted to check on you. Make sure you were okay since our last talk."

I nodded. "I'm feeling pretty good right now," I said as I brought the joint back to my lips for another hit.

"When did you start doing that?" Violet asked as she took a seat beside me.

I exhaled, choking at the end, before answering her. "It's recent."

"Can I?" Violet held her hand out for a hit.

"Uh...have you before?" I asked, uncertain of turning her on my bad habit.

She took it from me, taking a long drag while nodding. She exhaled before being enveloped in a coughing fit like I had. "Last year when I was going through that breakup. Scarlet gave me some, but now that she doesn't do it, she'll talk shit about anyone who does."

"I didn't know Scarlet smoked."

"She kept it pretty well hidden. I wouldn't have known if she hadn't given me some."

Bowie came closer and sat beside me. I had forgotten he was there. Violet reached across me and offered him the joint. He just waved his hand in a dismissive manner.

"Bowie doesn't smoke," I voiced.

Violet took another hit before handing it back to me.

"You should be careful doing that at school," Bowie stated.

I nodded. "It was probably a bad idea to do this here, huh?" I smirked at him.

He looked amused as he replied, "Yeah, definitely not your best idea."

"So, we hung out, and now you've been AWOL again. What's going on with you?" Violet asked.

I hesitated, looking down at the joint held between my fingers. I sighed before answering, "I ran into Osbourne the other day."

Bowie perked up. "You didn't tell me that."

I nodded and tried to keep the tears at bay. "It was last week. That's why I didn't come to school the rest of the week."

"You were at my house Monday. You didn't come back to school the next day, so you ran into him after you were at my house?" Violet asked.

I nodded. "I didn't want to go home, so I was just out walking around for a while. I ended up out on a cliff, looking over the sea. I guess he followed me because he showed up there."

"Did the two of you talk?" Bowie asked with a stern expression.

"More like argued."

"What about?" Bowie prodded while Violet sat quietly, listening.

"About what happened between us. About the misunderstanding. I told him that I was stupid for thinking he would surprise me and be there for me through everything I've been going through."

"What did he say when you said that?" Violet asked just above a whisper.

Tears slid down my cheeks as I shook my head. "He didn't say anything. He just let me walk away."

Bowie chuckled dryly. "He's an idiot."

I looked over at him, confused. "What do you mean?"

"He could've said something. He could've tried to fix things, to at least try to be a friend or a shoulder to cry on, but he didn't. He let you leave. He's an idiot for not trying."

I sniffled. "I thought you said it was better for me to navigate this on my own."

Violet snapped, "You told her what?! She just lost her parents and is grieving! She shouldn't be dealing with this alone!"

Bowie stared at her wide eyed. "Out of context! There was more to it than just that. What I told her was that not being in a new relationship might be for the best, because it's not healthy to use a partner as your source of happiness or as a distraction from dealing with your grief."

Violet huffed and nodded. "Yeah, okay. Those are good points and very true. But she shouldn't deal with this much trauma alone."

I chuckled at her protectiveness. "Don't worry, Vi. He's been a very supportive friend. I mean, he was the one with me when it happened after all."

"When what happened?" she asked.

"When I got the call that my parents were in the hospital. When they died."

"I didn't know that," she murmured.

After a silent moment, Bowie spoke again, "Back to what I was saying. Jack's an idiot for not trying."

"And why is that?" I asked again.

"Because the two of you don't need to be back where you were or in a relationship while you're going through this, but if he wanted another shot in the future, he should've tried to be a friend to you now, when you need support."

"He's right. Did he even ask how you're dealing with everything?"

I shook my head as the tears fell and mumbled, "No."

Bowie slid his arm around my shoulders and pulled me in a side hug, and Violet snaked her arm around my waist, scooting close to me. Tears continued to fall as they comforted me as my heart broke a little more.

"Dee," Violet whispered.

"Yeah?" I asked.

"Are you focusing so much on everything between you and Osbourne so that you don't have to think about your parents?"

Sobs began shaking my body as my head fell. Violet and Bowie, both, held me tighter as I cried. Neither of them said anything, and they just held me as I fell apart. After a few minutes of sobbing, I pulled myself together with shaky breaths. I used my sleeves to wipe my face.

"Guys?" I said in a quiet voice.

"Yeah?" they responded.

"I think I need to go live with my uncle."

Violet gripped me tighter, and she said in a sad voice, "Doesn't he live in California?"

A few more tears slipped down my face. "Yeah, but everything here is just too much. I think leaving for a while might be good for me. Earnest said that Nicholai will take me if I want to move out there."

"Earnest is your foster dad?" Violet clarified.

"Yeah," I mumbled as I nodded.

"Del," Bowie began, "do you want to leave because it will help you, or are you running from everything here?"

I was quiet as I thought about his question. "Honestly, it might be a bit of both. I just know that here, everything reminds me of my parents, and if it's not my parents, then I'm faced with Osbourne and reminded of that whole situation."

Bowie sighed. "Near, far, no matter where you are, I'm here for you."

Violet laughed and said, "I thought you were busting out Céline Dione lyrics for a second."

Bowie flipped her off. "I'm always a call or text away," he said to me.

The bell rang, signaling the end of the lunch period. The three of us stood up and made our way towards the school building. I stopped and pulled Violet and Bowie to a stop as well. I looked at Bowie and asked, "Can you tell we've been smoking?"

He hesitated before answering, "Violet's eyes are glassy as hell. It's obvious that you've been crying, so you don't really look high, just sad."

I rolled my eyes and huffed. "Great. I'd much rather look high than sad." I looked over at Violet in concern. "How are we going to cover up your stoned look?"

She waved her hand with a smile. "It's all good. I have eyedrops in my locker."

I giggled at her response and nodded. "Okay, that's good."

We continued our way to the lockers. I stopped them before we went our separate ways. "Do you guys wanna make cookies after school?"

Bowie smirked at me. "I was wondering when you were going to want to do that."

"I'm in!" Violet exclaimed.

"We can go to my house after school."

"Your mom won't mind?" I asked.

"Definitely not. She keeps asking when you'll be over again."

"Sweet!" Violet cheered.

We dispersed and headed to our lockers. After the lunch break I had, I was looking forward to having cookies. It was all I could think about the rest of the day.

Chapter 23

Violet, Bowie, and I met up in the parking lot after school, and Violet drove us to Bowie's house. Marissa had taken the car to work that morning and was picking up ingredients for us to make cookies on her way home.

Walking into Bowie's house, Violet looked all around before mumbling, "Nice house."

"Thanks," he mumbled back.

"How long before Marissa gets home?" I asked.

"Shouldn't be much longer," Bowie responded.

He was right. It wasn't much longer before Marissa came in with bags on each of her arms. Bowie was quick to help his mom while Violet and I stood nearby. Once Bowie had taken the bags from Marissa, she turned to me with a smile. She came over with open arms, pulling me into a hug.

"Delta, how've you been, Sweetheart?"

I hugged her back and mumbled, "I'm okay. How've you been?"

"Oh, just working all the time." She chuckled as she pulled away.

I motioned to Violet and said, "This is my friend, Violet. Vi, this is Bowie's mom, Marissa."

"It's nice to meet you, Violet," Marissa said as she pulled Violet into a hug.

Violet giggled and said, "It's nice to meet you too."

"As much as I'd love to stay and hang out with you kids, I have plans tonight."

I gave Marissa another hug and said, "Have fun."

"Don't let Bowie catch my kitchen on fire."

Violet and I laughed while Bowie rolled his eyes. "Don't worry, Marissa," Violet began. "We'll keep a close eye on him."

After she left, Violet turned to Bowie and said, "I like your mom."

"Yeah, she's alright," he replied.

The three of us made a mess of the kitchen, but ultimately, we had fun throwing ingredients all over each other while we made the cookie dough. We cleaned up the mess—except for what was in our hair and all over our clothes—while we waited for the cookies to bake. The three of us stepped outside to try to get some of the flour off. Violet broke out in a fit of giggles while she tried to help me dust off. Bowie just grumbled about how he would never do this again.

"Awwe, Bowie, don't say that," I pouted. "You know you'll want to do this with us again."

He looked at me with a stern expression. "Why on earth would I want to get covered in flour again?"

Violet smiled at him and said, "Because it makes us," she motioned to me and herself, "happy."

He rolled his eyes and grumbled, "Whatever."

After dusting off the best we could, the three of us went back inside. Once the cookies were done, we piled them on a plate and sat on the floor in the living room and turned the TV on. That was how we spent our evening. After a while, Violet announced that she needed to head home. She had offered me a ride home, but I didn't want to go home just yet. Bowie assured Violet that he would make sure that I got home safely whenever I was ready to go. After saying our goodbyes to Violet, Bowie and I stood in silence in the kitchen.

"Bowie, I want to ask you something, but I'll understand if you don't want to answer."

"What's your question?"

"How's Ozzie doing?"

Bowie sighed and turned to me. "Why are you asking me that, Delta?"

Tears rimmed my eyes, and I tried to push down the emotions threatening to spill out. "I just want to know...I..." I took a deep breath before speaking again, "I want him to be doing okay. A part of me wishes that he's falling apart too, but a bigger part of me wishes that he's doing okay."

Bowie sighed again and looked at me. "He's...he's doing the best he can. I can tell he's not sleeping much again. It's obvious that he misses you, but I think he's trying to go back to the way his life was before he met you."

I looked down and nodded as a few tears slipped down my cheeks. Bowie pulled me into a hug and held me tightly. "I wish things turned out differently," I whispered to him.

"I do too," he mumbled back.

Chapter 24

The morning after making cookies at Bowie's, I announced to Earnest and Evangeline that I had decided to move to California to live with Nicholai. An awkward tension seemed always to be present between me and them after that. I began spending less time in their home and more time out with Zen.

Normally, Zen would pick me up, and we would meet up with everyone else. Zen had some things to take care of at home that night, so Havoc and Jewel picked me up instead. I slipped into the backseat, and Havoc started driving. We pulled up to the park near Bowie's house, and Havoc parked. I climbed out of the car, and Jewel grabbed my hand and twirled herself around. I chuckled and let her dance around me as we walked to where everyone else would meet us.

"Hey," Tess drew out.

I smirked at her and wiggled my fingers in a wave. "Hi, Tess."

"So what are we doing tonight," Jewel asked as she twirled around.

"What we always do," Zen said, bringing all of our attention to him as he walked up to us.

"I figured when you said you'd be late, it was because you were going to be busy showing Delta a good time," Tess remarked.

I rolled my eyes and smacked her arm before turning to Zen. "Why were you late?"

He pulled a baggie out of his pocket and answered, "I had to pick up the grass."

We decided stargazing with a game of puff-puff-pass would be the perfect way to pass the time.

I took a hit off the joint offered to me, and it wasn't long before the affects took over me. I laid down in the grass and looked up at the stars. Numbness washed over me, and I smiled at the nothingness I felt. Nobody paid me much attention after I took the hit, and I was glad for that.

So much had changed in my life over the past six months, and it would only be one more month until I would move two states over. I was ready to leave everything behind and start over. I was tired of all the brokenness I felt. A fresh start would be the best thing for me. Better than the solution that I had come to at the cliff.

My thoughts and the feeling of nothingness were cut short when a familiar voice filled my ears. Even in my high state, I couldn't stop the tightness in my chest that I felt anytime he was near. I wanted to get up and leave. I wanted to disappear before he saw me. But I couldn't get up in the state I was in. My body felt too heavy to move, so I continue to lie where I was, staring up at the stars. I prayed he wouldn't notice me or come over to me. My prayers were denied.

"Hey, can we talk?" He stood above my head and crouched down closer to me.

I closed my eyes so that I wouldn't have to look at him. "I'd rather not."

He was quiet for a moment before asking, "How high are you?"

I opened my eyes and looked at him. I furrowed my eyebrows and snapped, "None of your damn business."

He ran a hand over his face. I took that moment to really look at him for the first time in weeks. He had dark circles under his eyes and looked far more tired than usual. I surprised him by reaching up and caressing his cheek. "Why aren't you sleeping?" I asked.

He cleared his throat. "I, uh...Does it matter?"

I chuckled dryly and let my hand drop back down beside me. "I guess not. Nothing really matters anymore, does it?"

"Why are being so cynical?"

"I'm not being cynical. I'm being realistic."

He stared at me in silence for a few moments. He cleared his throat and looked away from me. Just when I thought maybe he was done and would walk away, he looked back at me. "Is there anyway that we can fix things? I...I miss you. I miss my best friend."

My heart broke a little more hearing the emotion in his voice. I wanted to wrap my arms around him and kiss away any pain he was feeling. I wanted to be held by him. But that wasn't our reality anymore. I held back the many emotions rushing through me and answered him. "It's too late. I'll be leaving next month."

I could see the pain in his eyes as he processed this new information. "Where are you going?"

"I'm moving in with my uncle in California."

"Wow, California. That—uh, that's great. That, that will be great for you." And with that, he stood up and walked away.

I laid there, falling apart on the inside, knowing I broke the boy I was in love with.

Chapter 25

I didn't sleep the night Osbourne and I talked. I was up thinking about how broken he looked, how broken I felt. Something in me stirred, and I wished I hadn't been high when we talked. I wanted to talk to him again, to try to fix things. I wanted to tell him that I could always change my mind about going to California. I considered talking to him at school, but I couldn't think of a way it would turn out well.

I glanced down the hallway and saw him talking with Bowie and Arvin. Osbourne turned and looked in my direction, and I quickly looked away. Closing my locker door, I hurried to my first class. An anxious feeling flowed through me, and I had a bad feeling about how today would turn out.

The anxious feeling chewed at me, and by the time the last class before lunch ended, I felt sick to my stomach. I took a deep breath in an attempt to self-soothe. As I shut my locker, I jumped at the sudden realization that someone was standing beside me, and I yelped out, "Shit!"

"Sorry, I-I didn't mean to scare you."

I looked at Osbourne's tired face before quickly looking at my feet, my hair falling around my face. My heart raced, and I felt even more nauseous than before.

"Look, I don't want to make you upset, or-or make things any worse than they already are. I just...I wanted to talk to you last night, and it didn't go that well. I just...wanted to try again."

"I was too high for conversations last night," I mumbled back.

He ran his hand through his hair as he let out a shaky breath. "Yeah. Look, I just wanted to apologize for everything. I—I know I messed everything up, and I wasn't there when I should've been. I know I can't fix things now, but I don't..."

"'You don't,' what?"

"I don't know how to word this in a way that doesn't sound like a judgmental asshole."

I chuckled, "Just say it. I won't get mad or walk off without you explaining."

"I wish you wouldn't hang out with Zen and his friends."

I looked up at him. I really looked at him. His eyes dark, and he looked thinner. I sighed and looked away, crossing my arms over my chest. I looked back at him. "Bowie doesn't like me hanging out with them either."

"You've been hanging out with Bowie?"

I bit my lip and nodded. "He checks in on me. He tries to make sure I'm not doing anything too stupid."

"I'd rather you hang out with him than Zen."

I sighed. "Is this what you wanted to talk about?"

He shook his head and said, "No."

"Well...what did you want to talk about?"

He sighed and ran his hand through his hair. "I just...I know...I know everything is hard right now. I should've been there for you more through everything. I...I get why you want to get high, but it won't fix things. As much as I wish I had more time to try to fix things, I think going to California will be good for you. You'll get to start over."

Tears pricked my eyes, and I wrapped my arms around him. I buried my face in his chest as I shed a few tears. The hug was short lived, and I wiped my eyes as I stepped away and looked at him. "Ozzie, I'm happy we had what we did while we had it. I know there were times we both should've handled things better, but this, right now, I'm glad we're having this moment. My life was better with you in it."

"But you're still going to California."

I sighed. "I'm still going to California."

He smiled sadly. "I'm glad we could talk like this before that happened."

Tears spilled down my cheeks, and I quickly wiped them away. "I am too."

"I don't know why I was such an ass."

"Everything happens for a reason."

"And what reason did you find for me being an ass?"

I looked at him as sadness and pain washed over me. "It gave me something else to think about."

He pulled me into him and held me tightly as he said, "I should've been a shoulder for you, never a distraction."

"I know, but things don't always work out the way we think they should," I mumbled as I hugged him for the last time.

Pulling away from him, I felt a calmness wash over me. My chest didn't hurt when I looked at him, and for the first time in a long time, I felt like things might turn out okay. I should've known that that was the calm before the storm. That serene moment made me forget about the uneasiness that had followed me all day. I should've known things couldn't be so easy.

Walking into the cafeteria and towards the table that my friends sat at, that uneasiness came back. As I approached the table, Scarlet looked at me with a smug expression. I hesitated to sit down. Something in me knew that she was about to say something that would piss me off. I looked at her blankly as she stared back at me.

"What?"

"You let that loser back in your life quicker than I expected. Did losing your parents really make you that lonely?"

Something in me snapped. Before anyone could process what was happening, I was on top of Scarlet and hitting her. All the years of her backhanded comments and snide remarks were taken out on her in that moment. I could hear Violet begging me to stop and could feel someone grabbing at me, but I didn't care. It wasn't until someone wrapped their arms around my waist and picked me up off of Scarlet that I noticed the crowd around us. It wasn't until that moment that I felt the tears on my face. I pulled away from whoever had picked me up and realized it was Bowie. I hurried out of the cafeteria, ignoring everyone who was calling my name.

"Delta!" Bowie called out to me.

I stopped and turned to him, tears pouring down my face.

"What the hell was that? I know Scarlet can be a bitch, but what could she possibly say to piss you off that much?"

Sniffling, I said, "I guess she saw me and Ozzie talking before lunch, because she said something about losing my parents must've made me really lonely to take that loser back." As the words left my lips, more tears poured down my cheeks.

He sighed and pulled me into a hug. "If I'd known that, I would've let you keep beating her ass."

I hugged him back and chuckled. "How was I ever friends with such a nasty person?"

"Because you choose to see the good in people."

I shook my head and pulled away. "Not anymore."

"Hey—" before he could say anymore, I was called to the office.

"See you when I see you, I guess," I mumbled before turning in the direction of the office.

Chapter 26

It had been two days since I was suspended for the fight with Scarlet. Joshua, Violet, and Bowie have texted every day to check in on me. I barely left my room. Evangeline and Earnest let me know how disappointed they were in me for the fight. They didn't ask why I'd gotten into the fight, and I didn't feel obligated to talk to them about it.

They were both at work, and Zen texted me to see if I wanted to hang out. Of course, I took him up on his offer and met up with him and the others at the park.

"Oooo, skipping school today?" Havoc teased.

"Can't skip when you're suspended," I chuckled.

Zen looked up at me and asked, "You got suspended?"

I nodded while I watched Havoc roll a joint.

"What'd you do?" Tess asked.

I shrugged, not really wanting to discuss what happened, and nonchalantly said, "Got in a fight."

"Really, you got in a fight?" Zen asked.

"Yeah, so what?" I snipped.

He shook his head and said, "Nothing, it's just...surprising."

"Joint is ready. Who wants the first hit?"

I snatched it from him and cheered, "Me!"

He chuckled and lit the joint while I puffed. Before I could finish the hit, Zen exclaimed, "Shit!"

Before I knew what was happening, everyone was up and running, and I was being grabbed. I turned to be face-to-face with a cop. "Shit."

The officer raised his brow at me. "How old are you?"

"Would you believe me if I said twenty-one?"

He chuckled, "Not a chance."

I sighed. "I'm seventeen."

The second officer asked, "What's your name?"

"Delta Novak." The second officer had a strange expression cross his features when I said my name.

"Why aren't you in school, Ms. Novak?" The first officer asked.

"I'm suspended right now," I mumbled, knowing this wasn't going to end well for me.

"Troublemaker?"

"Not usually."

"What'd you get suspended for?"

"It wasn't pot, if that's what you're wandering."

The second officer cut in, "You wouldn't be related to Nikita and Lillian Novak, would you?"

A lump formed in my throat, and I nodded, unable to incite myself to speak.

"The couple in that terrible accident?" The first officer asked his partner.

Tears spilled down my cheeks, despite my attempts at pushing down my emotions. "Can we not talk about my parents?"

The officers both looked at me with pity. The first officer spoke again, "We'll have to take you in and call your guardian."

Sitting in that police station felt like an eternity. I was dreading my foster parents coming to pick me up. I didn't know what was going to happen to me, and I was worried that my uncle wouldn't take me if he found out I got in trouble with the police. So many thoughts went through my head as I sat, waiting to find out what was going to happen to me. Finally, Earnest walked in.

He sat across from me with that disappointed expression on his face.

"Can you not look at me like that?"

"Like what?"

"Like I just killed your cat."

"I don't have a cat."

I scrunched up my eyebrows and tilted my head to the side.

Earnest sighed and began again, "I know things are hard for you, but you need to get your shit together for the remainder of the time you'll be with us."

Hearing the word "shit" from a man I'd never heard swear before was unsettling. Nervousness ate at me as I avoided eye contact. I stayed silent, and he sighed again.

"They said you'll be on house arrest until you leave for California if you tell them who the marijuana belonged to."

"So they want me to be a snitch?"

"Delta, you're a good kid going through a bad time. Whoever the pot belonged to isn't your friend. The officer told me that the people you were with ran and left you there."

Tears pricked my eyes. He was right. I wasn't their friend. I was some girl who had stumbled upon them one day, and they were too stoned to turn me away. They didn't know me, and they didn't care about me. Not really.

I nodded my head as the tears fell, and I said, "I'll tell them. I just know their first names, though. Will that be enough?"

"It should be."

Chapter 27

I was put on house arrest, and I was permitted to continue my schoolwork online. The days would drag, and I was constantly left alone with thoughts of my parents. I no longer had pot to distract me, and Osbourne and I were on better terms. I couldn't avoid dealing with my parents' deaths anymore.

I would sob until I felt like I couldn't breathe, and my dreams were often filled with them—happy and alive. I would wake up and be reminded of the horrible truth of them being gone. I was miserable, but I was finally dealing with losing them. I was facing it instead of running away. As much as it hurt to face it, I was.

My days were mostly spent alone until my foster family came home. Even then, I felt alone. I still felt like a piece to a different puzzle. I was counting down the days to my move to California.

The start to that day wasn't any different. I spent the day turning in assignments, and then I cried until I had no tears left. Eventually, Phoenix came home, and I happened to be coming down the stairs, headed for the kitchen. I felt like making cookies. Phoenix passed me and was headed up the stairs when I turned and called his name.

He stopped and turned. "What do you want?"   I hesitated, rethinking what I was about to ask. I let out a breath and forced the words out. "Do you want to make cookies with me?"

His eyebrows furrowed together as he looked down at me. "Cookies?"

"Uhh...it's stupid. Never mind," I mumbled quickly, backing out on the invite.

"No, wait," he called as he came down the stairs towards me. "I'll make cookies with you. I just didn't expect you to ask me that."

I smiled at him. "Thanks, Phoenix."

He shrugged and mumbled, "If Destiny gets home soon, she can help."

I nodded beside him as we walked into the kitchen.

Destiny didn't get home in time to help make the cookies, but we promised to let her help put the next batch on the cookie sheet. In the meantime, she was playing in her room, and Phoenix and I were hanging out in the kitchen.

"So why did you want to make cookies?"

I looked over at him. I hesitated to answer. Finally, I took a deep breath and told him. "My mom used to make cookies with me when I was sad or upset."

He looked at me with furrowed brows. "You wanted to make cookies because you're sad?"

I nodded and looked away. I could feel the tears forming in my eyes, and I tried to push the emotions down. "It's...it's been really hard...losing my parents. I was really close with them."

"You know, we would've been your family, if you'd have let us."

I looked at him, sadness washing over me. "I don't fit in here, Phoenix. You have a wonderful family, but it just reminds me of what I lost."

He was quiet for a moment before he asked, "Did you have any siblings?"

I shook my head. "Nope. No siblings."

"It was always just you and your parents?"

I nodded. "Just the three of us."

"Are you close to your uncle? The one you're going to live with?"

I looked at him. "No. The first time I officially met him was at my parents' funeral."

"So you're going to move to another state to live with a man you don't know because it's too hard to live here?"

I wiped the tears that started running down my cheeks. "Yup."

Phoenix did something I never expected him to do. He walked over to me and hugged me. "If you decide you don't like living with him, I'm sure Mom and Dad will let you come back here."

I wrapped my arms around him and began sobbing on his shoulder. I had done nothing but push this family away, and here was this kid making me feel welcomed and loved despite all that I'd said and done.

The rest of that night was spent laughing with Phoenix and Destiny while we made and ate cookies. I finally was feeling like myself again and that I might make it through. Even though I was broken without my parents, I was going to be okay.

Chapter 28

The days went by in a blur of schoolwork, crying, and spending time with my foster family. Before I knew it, it was time to have the ankle monitor removed, and I had to start packing for California. I would be flying out two days.

Evangeline came to my room to help me pack. An uncomfortable silence fell between us as we did so. We hadn't spent much time alone together. Just as I was beginning to think packing with her would be unbearable, she broke the silence.

"Earnest and I are so happy for the time we got with you."

I looked over at her hesitantly. "I did nothing but cause trouble for you."

"That's not true. These past few weeks, you really opened up to us. Phoenix and Destiny have loved the time they've had with you. They really think of you as a sister."

I stopped what I was doing and looked over at her. "But I'm not their sister. I'm leaving."

She shook her head. "It doesn't matter where you are, you have a home here, with us." She looked up at me and continued, "You've had your bad moments, but you're just a kid who lost too much too early."

Tears filled my eyes, and my chest tightened. "Does Earnest feel the same?"

She nodded. "You're always welcome here. I hope things go well for you in California, but if you ever want to come back here, you can. You can always visit, too."

I wrapped my arms around her and began crying into her shoulder. She returned the hug and rested her chin on my head. "It's okay, Delta."

"Thank you. Thank you for being so nice to me, even when I didn't make it easy."

"That's what family's for." She pulled away and wiped my tears away. "Now, let's hurry and get everything packed, and we can start planning a small going-away party for tomorrow."

I smiled at her. "A party for our little family?"

She nodded and said, "And any of your friends."

My smile grew. "I can have my friends over?"

"Of course. I don't want you to leave without seeing them first."

"Thanks, Evangeline."

She smiled at me and said, "Of course."

Chapter 29

E vangeline kept her word and let me have a small party. I invited Marco, Joshua, Violet, Bowie, Arvin, and Osbourne. While awaiting the guests, Phoenix and I kept busy cleaning and fixing food. He and I decided we wanted to have one last time cooking together, but Evangeline wanted the house to look nice for the guests. It was a small party with simple foods, but Evangeline seemed nervous about having my friends over.

"Don't worry, Del. Mom always freaks over meeting our friends."

I looked over at Phoenix. "What do you mean?"

"She's always afraid they won't like her. She likes making a good impression on people."

I chuckled. "Trust me, my friends will like her just fine."

"Hey," he began, looking nervous.

"What's up?"

"Okay, don't take this the wrong way, but you didn't invite the people you were with when you got arrested, did you?"

I smiled at him. "No. I didn't invite any of them."

He sighed. "Good."

"When I sat in that interrogation room with your dad, he was right when he said those people weren't my friends. They just left, and I was the one who got caught."

"What a bunch of shitheals."

I laughed harder than I had in a long time. "What the hell, Phoenix?"

"What? That's what Dad calls the people he doesn't like at work."

I smiled at him. "Well, maybe don't call people that around your parents, and definitely don't say that in front of Destiny."

He shrugged and mumbled, "Okay."

We pulled the first pizza out of the oven when the doorbell rang.

"I'll get it!" Evangeline called as she made her way to the door.

She quickly led Marco and Joshua into the kitchen. I smiled and wiggled my fingers at them. "Hi, Marco. Hi, Joshy."

The boys smiled back and said, "Hi, Del."

"I'm glad you guys could make it."

"Wouldn't miss it for the world," Joshua commented.

"I don't know about that. The world is a big place, and there's lots of things in the world. I mean, Del's great and all, but there's lots of things in the world."

Joshua smacked Marco on the back of the head and mumbled, "Shut up."

I chuckled at them and hurried over to them, pulling them into a group hug. "I'm going to miss you idiots."

"We're going to miss you, too," Joshua mumbled into me.

"Great, you guys are being all sweet and cuddly without me."

I pushed the boys away to squeeze the life out of Violet. "Vi! I've really missed you."

She laughed and hugged me back. "I've missed you too, Novak."

We pulled apart, and she shook her head at me. "You're really leaving us all behind, and it's not even graduation yet. Overachiever."

I smiled at her sadly. "Well, you're the luckiest girl in the world because there's no way in hell I'm not keeping in touch with you."

Tears filled her eyes as she pulled me in for another hug. "I'm going to miss you so much."

I whimpered out, "I'm going to miss you too."

"If I knew this was going to be such an emotional thing, I would've skipped it."

"Shut up, Bowie," Violet yelled at him.

I laughed and pulled away from Violet. I turned to Bowie, who stood with an awkward looking Arvin. "Don't think you're getting out of here without a hug, Newton."

He rolled his eyes before asking, "Are you going to make us all make cookies or is this going to be more of a hanging out, happy thing?"

"I don't know how happy it'll be, but I'm not making anyone make cookies."

"Yeah, we did that last night," Phoenix yelled out.

Bowie laughed and walked over to me. He stood in front of me for a moment before pulling me into a hug. "I'm just going to rip this Band-Aid off really quick. Jack wanted to be here, but he said that he couldn't handle saying goodbye again. I just think he's afraid of messing things up again."

I held Bowie tightly at the mentioning of Osbourne. "That's okay. I wasn't sure if he'd come. I'm glad you bothered to show up, though."

"I know we didn't start off on good terms, but I can't imagine my life without you in it. You're a good friend, and I'm going to miss you."

I buried my face in his should as the tears began pouring. "I'm really going to miss you. I mean, who's going to tell me when I'm being a dumbass?"

"Well, there's always texting and phone calls. FaceTime."

I chuckled into him.

"We can always bake cookies over video chat."

I sniffled and mumbled, "I'd really like that."

I pulled away and looked at him. "I never thought you'd be someone I'd miss so much."

He smiled sadly and said, "I never thought you'd be someone I'd miss either."

I looked beside him. "I'm sorry you feel so awkward, Arvin. I know we weren't really close, but I'm glad you came."

He smirked at me, "I wouldn't miss out on saying bye to someone who knocked Bowie's ass into the ocean."

I laughed at the day he was referring to. "So much has happened, I'd forgotten about that."

Arvin grabbed my arm and pulled me into a hug. "I'm sorry I stopped talking to you after you and Jack split."

"It's okay. I had a lot going on anyways."

The rest of the evening was spent with reminiscence, laughter, and tears. Earnest and Evangeline permitted anyone with parental approval to stay over if they wanted. Bowie and Violet were the only ones to stay over, and we set up camp in the living room with snacks and movies.

Violet was the first to fall asleep. It was after midnight, and Bowie and I were still going strong. Bowie went to get more snacks from the kitchen when he stopped to look out the window.

"Del, someone's sitting on the sidewalk outside your house."

"What?!" I exclaimed and rushed over to him. "Can you tell who that is?"

He shrugged and said, "No clue." He walked over to the door and began unlocking it.

I smacked his shoulder and snapped, "What are you doing?"

He turned to face me, looking slightly annoyed. "Don't you want to find out who it is?"

I debated it for a moment before nodding. "Yeah, but we shouldn't get too close in case it's a crazy person."

He rolled his eyes and mumbled, "Whatever."

We quietly slipped outside and cautiously walked toward the figure. As we crept closer, I realized who was sitting there. "Zen?"

He turned around and looked between mc and Bowie before standing up and walking towards us. "Hey, haven't heard from you in a while."

"Uh...yeah." I looked at the ground, refusing to make eye contact with him.

"Look, I know we shouldn't have split the way we did in the park, but we all panicked."

Bowie scoffed and muttered, "Yeah."

I glanced at him then looked up at Zen. "It doesn't matter anymore, Zen."

"You have every right to be upset with us, but we all miss you. You won't return any of our texts."

"I'm leaving."

"What?"

"I'm moving to California to live with my uncle. You haven't seen me around because I've been under house arrest. You haven't heard from me because sitting in that police station made me realize that you and the others weren't my friends. You guys just left me there, and it was a week before any of you even texted to check on me."

Zen nodded and said, "I'm sorry you feel that way."

I shook my head and looked away. "That's what you're sorry about."

"You're a real douchebag," Bowie cut in.

"Bowie," I said sternly, grabbing his arm. "It's fine. Don't worry about it."

I sighed. "I'm not sorry I met you. It was a life lesson meeting you and the others. Goodbye, Zen."

I turned, grabbed Bowie's hand, and dragged him away with me. Once we were back in the house, I leaned back against the door and sighed. "I didn't expect him to show up."

"Hey, Del?"

I looked over at Bowie. "Yeah?"

"Any reason you're still holding my hand?" Bowie asked, lifting our hands, fingers still entwined.

I felt my cheeks warm up and quickly released his hand. "Sorry," I mumbled.

He laughed at my awkwardness. "Don't worry about it, Del." He sighed and rubbed the back of his neck. "You know, I'm really going to miss you."

I looked at him sadly. "I'm really going to miss you too."

He and I spent the rest of the night watching movies, trying our hardest to stay awake. I think we both wanted to savor what little time we had left together. I remember thinking, as I drifted off to sleep, that with all the changes I'd gone through that year, I didn't know if I'd ever find a better friend than Bowie had been.

Epilogue

I sat on the plane, nervousness filling me as I waited to take off to California. I thought back to the people who came to see me the day before. The precious friends I'd had—the people I was leaving behind. I'd made a mess of my life, but here I was, moving towards a fresh start. While my friends, family, and I all agreed that a fresh start was what I needed, I couldn't help but long for the people I was now leaving behind. I thought back to each person and how much they meant to me.

I'd changed so much in such a short period of time, and I had finally begun fixing the mess I'd made after losing my parents. A part of me wished I'd stayed to keep fixing things, but life isn't about everything being perfect. Some things stay broken, and sometimes we just have to walk away. It's just the way we say "Goodbye."